To my friend and guide, Ed Mahoney, once
of Leesburg, now of Salmon, Idaho

CHAPTER
ONE

The daily stage for Salmon City left the Red Rock railhead at seven in the morning, heading west toward the Bitterroot divide. It would be a twelve-hour run with five team changes. The first leg was fairly level and Jake Slavin whipped his animals to a gallop.

"He'll wind 'em!" a passenger worried.

"Or bust a wheel!" another complained. The coach lurched recklessly.

"Maybe he's got a reason." A third passenger narrowed his eyes shrewdly. "Folks seemed kind of excited, back there at Red Rock. Like somebody was shot up and needs a doctor. You notice it, young fella?"

The youngest man in the coach, Dave Harbison, said, "It's a telegram, I think. Just before we left, the depot operator came running to the driver with it."

"It's sure buildin' a fire under him. You'd think Indians were chasin' him." This from a paunchy cattle buyer named Whipple. While waiting at the stage depot Dave Harbison had learned their names. The other two were Fred Brinker, a clerk at the Lemhi Indian agency, and a Salmon City assayer named Mitchell. Harbison, who'd spent the past year in southern Idaho, was the

1

only passenger who was strange to the Salmon River country.

Ten minutes ahead of schedule the stage rolled into Horse Prairie station. Dave got out to stretch his legs while a hostler untraced four lathered horses and brought up fresh ones.

"Mind if I ride upstairs?" Dave asked, and at a nod of assent climbed to a seat beside the driver.

A whip snapped and they were off at a gallop, the coach swaying, Jake Slavin biting grimly on a short-stemmed pipe.

"If it's no secret, where's the fire?" Dave asked. He'd been west long enough to know you didn't press horses like this without a reason.

"It's no secret," the driver said. "Reckon everybody at Red Rock knows it by this time. And every operator on the Utah Northern must've heard that wire go through."

"A wire from who?"

"From the governor at Boise to the sheriff at Salmon City."

"About what?"

"A hangin'. They were buildin' the scaffold when I left Salmon City, day before yesterday mornin'."

"You mean the governor wired a reprieve?"

"Amounts to that. The official paper with his John Henry on it'll come along by train in time to catch tomorrow's stage for Salmon. This wire" — Jake tapped the edge of a yellow envelope showing at his shirt pocket — "says it's on the way and to call off the hangin'."

2

"When's it set for?"

"Ten o'clock tomorrow mornin'. We're due there at seven tonight, which gives us fifteen hours leeway."

Except for this warning telegram, Dave calculated, the reprieve itself would arrive nine hours too late. He knew that Red Rock was the nearest rail and telegraph point to the far-isolated county seat town of Salmon City, deep in the central Idaho gold country, and that Salmon's most direct contact with the outside world was this daily stagecoach bringing mail and passengers across the Bitterroot range. "What's the man's name, Jake? The one waiting to be hanged."

"Fella named Court Grady." Jake's horses had slowed to a walk and he whipped them to a run again.

"Why risk winding them," Dave protested, "when you've got fifteen hours to spare?"

"Every minute counts," the driver insisted. His long whip snapped again over four running horses.

"I guess good news oughta be ridden with spurs," Dave admitted, "when a man's sweating it out in a death cell."

Jake gave a snort. "It's not Grady I'm whippin' up for, but that purty little gal of his who came out here to stand by at his trial. She's still in town, writin' letters to the governor, pullin' every string she can. Last I saw of her she was standin' on the hotel porch starin' across at that hang-tree in the jailyard. The look on her face was somethin' I never want to see again. And if I can take it off o' there one minute quicker . . . Giddap!" The snapper cracked again as the stage rocked turbulently on.

When they pulled into Frying Pan, the second change station, the station man fixed a rebuking stare. "What are you tryin' to do, Jake? Kill 'em?" The horses were sweat-streaked and quivering.

Jake explained in an undertone and it made all the difference. In less than three minutes four strong fresh horses stood in the traces and the coach moved on toward Lemhi Pass.

"Eight miles to the next change," Jake told Dave. "Four up and four down."

Cedar closed about the trail and then pine. A plodding walk was the best gait possible. Dave caught the driver's mood and found himself leaning forward, impatiently, as though the very bend of his shoulders could speed the pace. He knew nothing of Court Grady or the crime for which he'd been condemned; what mattered was to cut short a cruel torment pinching the heart of a girl, bring relief to her agony of dread as she waited with a doomful deadline only a day away.

"She ain't much bigger'n a minute," Jake muttered, "and she's took about all she can take. Damn this grade, anyway!" He scowled at the upwinding trail ahead.

On and up, through a thickening forest, the stage moved sluggishly. Twice before the summit Jake had to rest the horses. At the second halt Dave jumped to the ground and coaxed the other passengers out of the stage. "Let's lighten the load," he suggested. When he explained why, they walked behind the coach for the rest of the climb, Mitchell and Brinker cheerfully, the

4

paunchy Whipple grudgingly. It took eight hundred pounds off the load during the last steep summit pull.

"Thanks," Slavin said when they were on top.

It was the continental divide, eight thousand feet above the sea, and from here it would be downhill every foot of the way to Salmon City. The sun was now noon high. As Slavin waited for the horses to stop blowing, Dave looked curiously at a sign tacked on a tree by the trail. The sign said:

LEMHI PASS

Lewis and Clark passed here, in the year 1805, guided by a Shoshoni girl named Sacajawea

"Giddap!" Using his brake cautiously, Jake started downhill at a tight-reined trot.

Timber on this western slope was lodgepole pine. Slavin slowed expertly for the curves and at the first long straightaway glanced curiously at the young stranger beside him. He saw brown eyes in a smooth tanned face, a lean loose frame rigged in flannel and corduroy. The high-crowned range hat was fairly new and although Dave Harbison wore a gunbelt, the belt had no gun or holster. The gun, Jake surmised, could be in his baggage. About twenty-two years old, Jake concluded; an eastern boy, likely, who'd come west not more than a year ago.

"One way you look at it," Dave Harbison said with a half bitter twist of his lips, "her case is kinda like mine. Only I got here too late."

"Too late for what?" Jake asked.

"Too late to help my brother. He was Gregg Harbison. Did you know him?"

Jake shook his head. But the name seemed vaguely familiar. He waited for more but Dave retreated to a shell of silence. As the stage rattled on down the grade Jake probed his memory.

After a dozen more twists of the trail it came back to him — a news story from Hailey, down in southern Idaho. Two years ago a man named Gregg Harbison had been found shot dead on his placer claim near Hailey, and the case had never been solved.

They hit the head of Agency Creek and pulled up at the halfway house, known as the Cold Spring station. Today's eastbound stage had already arrived and its passengers were inside eating. It was an hour past noon. "Make it quick," Jake shouted to Bill Sunderlin, the station master. "We got no time to fool around." He flashed a telegram and explained what it meant.

Sunderlin cupped his hand and yelled to the corral. "Finish graining those horses and slap on the harness. Jake's in a hurry."

He turned to the driver. "You might as well eat, Jake. If we'd known you were in a rush we'd've had the team ready."

Slavin and his passengers went in to a sage hen dinner. At another table the eastbound passengers were being served dessert. Outside their coach was ready to go. But when Sunderlin explained why Jake was in a hurry they lingered to fire questions. Everyone in the county knew about an execution scheduled in Salmon City the next day. This place had a bar and rooms for

6

transients. A pair of prospectors came in from the bar. The story of a reprieve telegram buzzed from lip to lip, drawing a strayman and a wolfer from the corrals. They bunched around Slavin to hear more about a telegram from Boise.

"Is it a stay of execution, Jake, or an out-and-out pardon?"

It was thirty-day stay, Jake thought. The telegram was sealed and he knew only what the depot operator had told him.

"Maybe it's a fake," the eastbound driver suggested. "Maybe the governor didn't send it. Maybe some pal of Grady's, down south, filed a wire just to get him off."

To Dave it didn't make sense. A trick like that would be too easily and quickly discovered. Presently the eastbound passengers trooped out and Dave heard their coach move up-trail toward the pass. One by one the others left, Jake waiting impatiently for his fresh horses. Dave heard a clink of trace chains as they were led to the front.

"Let's roll," Jake said.

They boarded briskly and moved off downcreek at a trot, Dave again sharing the top seat with Jake. "How far to Salmon City?"

"From here it's thirty-four miles," Jake said. "We change teams twice, at Tendoy and Baker's ranch."

Dave's watch said half past one. With a water grade all the way they should make it in five more hours.

Four miles below Sunderlin's the trail crossed Agency Creek at a gravel ford. A thick growth of pine hid the sun. Jake had to ease slowly through the ford and as his wheels cleared the water a masked rider appeared from the forest gloom. His rifle held an aim at Jake's head. "It's my drop, driver," he warned.

Slavin was the only armed man on the stage. A carbine was booted near his left elbow and his right hip had a forty-five. A reach for either would cost his life. "But you're wastin' your talents, fella," Jake said as he raised his hands. "I'm not haulin' enough gold dust this trip to wad a ten-gage shell with."

"Hop down," the rider snapped. He cocked the rifle. "You guys in the coach — get out with your hands up."

Slavin had no choice. He jumped to the ground and Dave did the same. The masked man, Dave noticed, had a brushy chin. Out of the coach, completely cowed, came Mitchell, Whipple and Brinker. Whipple took a fat wallet from his pocket and tossed it furtively into creekbank weeds.

The hold-up man took Jake's six-gun and rifle. He made sure the others weren't armed. "From here on you walk," he anounced. "Get out in front, everybody! Driver, you lead the team and go where I say."

His cocked rifle kept its aim on Jake. "Turn to the left," he ordered, "and head up that hollow."

A dim trail led up a narrow, tributary ravine. Jake Slavin, with a hand on the ring of a bridle bit, walked up that trail leading the horses. Trace chains clinked as the stage bumped along. In a minute the lodgepole pines hid them from the stage road.

The masked man with the brushy chin, keeping to his saddle, made the four passengers walk a little in advance of Slavin. Dave assumed they were being taken

8

out of hearing from the stage road so that they could be robbed at leisure.

"Grab what we got and get goin' with it!" Jake said bitterly.

"Keep walkin'." The man punched Jake with his rifle.

A sapling windfall blocked the ravine. "Drag it aside," the man snapped.

Dave, with the help of Mitchell and Brinker, heaved on the sapling and dragged it out of the way. Then they moved on, leading the four-horse stagecoach deeper and deeper into the woods.

A mile from the stage road the ravine widened. Dave saw a rude log cabin with a dugout provision cellar by it. A small pole corral was empty. Tools and scattered ore samples suggested the occupancy of a prospector.

"Unharness," the rifleman commanded, "and put the horses in the corral."

While Jake obeyed, Dave got in a word with him. "Who lives here, Jake?"

"It's a trapper's shack; but he only uses it in the winter. Right now a pick and shovel man named Smiley's sleepin' here. He'll likely show up before nightfall."

When the stage horses were corraled, the rifleman marched them to the dugout cellar. Its roof was a mound of clay, its entrance steep steps under an oblique door. The door was thief-proof, made of three-inch oak and equipped with hasp and padlock. "Down you go!" the masked man ordered.

It was not till they'd been herded into the dugout that Dave realized they weren't going to be robbed. "I'm padlockin' you in," the man called down.

"For how long?" The question came in a panic from Whipple.

"If we don't get out," Jake Slavin warned, "you'll swing for it. It's cold-blood murder if we starve down here!"

"You'll get out," the masked man promised confidently. "When Smiley comes home in the morning, bang on the door and he'll let you out."

The door slammed shut and Dave heard a padlock snap. He groped to the top of the steps and pushed upward mightily. The slanting oak planks wouldn't give.

In the darkness he couldn't see the others. A puzzled query came from the assayer, Mitchell. "Wonder why he didn't grab our pokes! I got sixty dollars on me."

Dave had the answer but Jake beat him to it. "Only one reason I can think of," the driver muttered. "He wasn't after our dough. All he wants is to make sure they don't call off that hangin' party, at ten in the mornin'."

There was a minute of hollow silence. It was broken by the agency clerk, Brinker. "But you said the governor sent a reprieve!"

"The sheriff at Salmon ain't heard about it yet," Slavin reminded him. "And unless we bust out of here he won't till it's too late!"

Nothing else made sense. They'd been waylaid to prevent the delivery of a reprieve — and to insure the execution of Court Grady.

CHAPTER
TWO

Yet to Dave the situation didn't seem hopeless. "Look, Jake," he argued. "You say there's two more change stations this side of Salmon. When you don't show up they'll come scouting for you, won't they?"

"I wouldn't bank on it," Jake gloomed. "It's supposed to be a daily stage but sometimes we cancel a run. Might be because there's not enough mail or express or passengers to make the trip pay; or maybe a stage horse goes lame or a coach needs a new wheel. Last week we missed a run just because a driver overate and had a bellyache. When I don't show up at Tendoy and Baker, nobody'll lose any sleep over it."

"Let's all push on the door," Brinker suggested.

Only two at a time could squeeze up the narrow, steep steps and after a session of pushing they gave up. Jake groped for a rock or a pry tool but found only a sack of rotting potatoes.

"Looks like we're stuck here till morning," Mitchell said.

"If Smiley's off panning gravel somewhere," Dave questioned, "why won't he show up before dark and let us out?"

"Because I heard talk of him," the assayer told them, "when we stopped for dinner at Sunderlin's. Smiley's in a room there sleeping off a binge. It's something he does regular, about once a month."

A glum conclusion came from Brinker. "That's what the hold-up man said: he said Smiley'd be home in the morning and let us out."

Whipple spoke fretfully from the dark. "But how could he know about Smiley's binge unless he was there himself?"

"He wouldn't know about the telegram," Mitchell put in, "unless he heard us talk about it."

"Narrows it down," Jake Slavin concluded. "He must be someone who was hangin' around Sunderlin's. Somebody who knows Smiley'll wake up sober and broke, in the mornin', with no place to go but home. It oughta get us outa here by nine a.m."

Which would be too late, Dave calculated, to stop the hanging in town. The distance was thirty miles — a four-hour ride on a fast horse.

The dugout was cold and damp. "We'll freeze," Whipple whimpered, "penned up in this hole all night!"

"Stop feelin' sorry fer yourself," Jake growled, "and start thinkin' about Court Grady. Why would anyone want him hanged?"

The assayer had a thought. "Grady was convicted of a killing. If he's not guilty, someone else is. The guilty man might figure that with Grady executed, the case would be washed up for good."

"But it wouldn't," Jake argued. "No matter what happens to us, the official reprieve, signed and sealed, 'll be along on tomorrow's stage. It'll bust the case wide open and set the whole county on a manhunt for whoever held us up."

Dave brooded over it a minute, then offered: "Maybe Grady knows something and doesn't know he knows it. I mean maybe he doesn't figure it's important. If he dies it dies with him. But if he lives he might some day tell about it."

Dave couldn't see the others but he could feel them staring skeptically in the dark. "Such as what?" Brinker prodded.

"Your guess is as good as mine," Dave said. "But lots of little things happen in a man's life that he doesn't bother to mention. For instance, as my train came through Blackfoot yesterday I saw a man on the depot platform with a brace of mallards and a shotgun. It wouldn't occur to me to tell a sheriff about it. But suppose that if I ever did happen to mention it, somebody would get in bad trouble!"

He could tell by the silence that no one was impressed. And except as a pattern, neither was Dave himself.

A match flared. It was Mitchell looking at his watch. "Half past three," he announced.

Which meant eighteen to twenty hours before they could expect Smiley to come soddenly home from Sunderlin's.

"What if we can't make him hear us?" Whipple fretted. "Him with a fat-headed hangover!"

"He won't be too fat-headed," Jake said, "to see four stage horses in the corral."

"And a deserted stage," Dave added. "Not to mention a padlock on his dugout door. He'll find us all right — about four hours too late."

A sardonic laugh came from Mitchell. "I'll be in no shape for that bear hunt, day after tomorrow."

"What bear hunt?" Brinker asked.

"Chuck Spoffard's taking a party up Geerston Creek. Some grizzly sign up there. But to hell with it! Let's talk about that hold-up man. A brushy chin and a brown corduroy coat, I remember."

Dave listened absently as they discussed the possibilities. More than a dozen men had been at Sunderlin's during the dinner stop. A strayman, a wolfer, a pair of prospectors, the driver and passengers of an eastbound stage, a barkeeper, waiter, cook, hostlers and wranglers, perhaps a few unseen room guests other than Smiley, as well as Sunderlin himself.

"Somebody was campin' across the creek," Jake remembered. "The trees hid him but I saw the smoke of his fire."

Dave tried to imagine any one of those men masking himself, then riding to a downcreek ford to hold up a stage. None seemed to fit the part.

Again a match flared and someone said it was four o'clock. The minutes were crawling. "Look, Jake," Dave said. "We've got nothing but time so let's use it. Tell us just what case they built against Grady and maybe it'll tie in with someone we saw at Sunderlin's."

"It's a tight case," Slavin said. "Two eyewitnesses, both honest as daylight. They swear they saw Grady shoot and rob Whitey Parks."

14

"Who was Parks?"

"He had a placer claim at Leesburg, west over the hump from Salmon. Couple of months ago he traded it for three thousand dollars' worth of gold dust and headed for the bright lights. Stayed a couple of nights in Salmon and did a lot of celebratin' there. By the time he moved on, everyone in town knew he had a poke of dust."

"Did he leave Salmon by stage?"

"Nope. He left by saddle leading a pack and headed up Lemhi Creek toward Nicolia. Said he had a cousin at Nicolia he aimed to stop a while with, then trail on to hit the railroad at Blackfoot. Ten miles upcreek from Salmon, Whitey must've passed Court Grady's little ranch. Grady claimed he didn't stop, and maybe he didn't. By nightfall we know Whitey got to the Dan Richmire homestead, thirty miles up the Lemhi from Salmon. The Richmires gave him supper but they've only got one bed in that cabin. So Whitey made camp across the creek. When the Richmires turned in they could see his campfire sparking not more'n sixty yards from their window."

"You say they're reliable, these Richmires?"

In the dark Dave couldn't see Jake's nod but the man's tone was crisply decisive. "Both of them past sixty, sweet as honey and gentle as pigeons."

Mitchell confirmed it. "Dan Richmire's a retired preacher. His wife Annie's just like him. Salt of the earth, both of them."

"Where," Dave prompted, "does Court Grady come in?"

"About daylight," Jake told him, "a gunshot woke up the Richmires. They jumped outa bed and looked from the window. At Whitey's camp they saw two men instead of only one. One of 'em had a smoky gun and he'd just shot Whitey. The Richmires saw him grab a poke, jump on a horse and make off. It was a man named Grady, they said, who had a place twenty miles nearer town. They had a good look at his face, they said."

The agency clerk, Brinker, struck a match and reported the time. Four-forty. A slight sound came from outside and Dave took it for the restless champing of a horse. "They'll need feeding before morning, Jake."

"So'll we," the driver growled. "We'll be spittin' cotton down here without any water." In that respect the stage horses were better off. The corral had a barrel of rain water.

Dave asked, "Did they find the poke of dust on Grady?"

"No — but he had plenty of time to get home and bury it somewhere. It took the Richmires all morning to hitch up a spring wagon and report the crime. And still more time before the sheriff could pick up Grady at his ranch. Grady claimed an alibi witness but couldn't prove it. He said a stranger had stopped by his place, about sunup, to ask the way to Haystack Mountain. Nobody else ever saw that stranger. The sheriff figgered Grady made him up. Grady's forty-five gun had been fired; said he'd knocked over a jackrabbit with it. He was stood in front of the Richmires and they said it was him all right."

16

"People past sixty," Dave suggested, "wear glasses. They take 'em off when they go to bed. You say this old couple jumped out of bed and looked through a window. They wouldn't see much, would they, without their specs?"

"At sixty yards, yes," Jake said. "They've got good far vision and use specs only to read. Lots of old folks are like that. I'm the same way myself. At the trial the prosecutor had 'em look from a courtroom window and pick out ten men across the street. They named 'em all. The killer took off on a bay horse, they said; and Grady owned a bay."

"A common color," Dave murmured. "What about Grady's past record?"

"Nothin' wrong with it, far as we know."

"Was he hard up for money?"

"He wanted to stock his place with grade heifers; tried to borrow money for it but the bank turned him down. So did all the other money lenders in the county. Grady was pretty sore about it. The prosecutor claims he went after that money with a gun."

"You can't buy cattle," Dave argued, "with a poke of dust you have to keep buried. Isn't that right, Mr. Whipple?"

But the cattle buyer was thinking only of himself. Mention of a poke made him remember his own. "Wonder if that guy saw me ditch it in a weed patch!" he fretted.

"Chances are he didn't," Slavin said. "He was busy reaching for my gun about that time. You can pick your money up on the way out of here."

"If we *ever* get out of here! What if that bum Smiley don't come home!"

Dave wriggled to a corner and sat with his back to a clay wall. By midnight it would be too cold to sleep; so if he slept at all it had better be now. He folded his arms and let his chin sag. An hour of silence dragged by. Toward the end of it Dave Harbison dozed for a while and the next voice he heard was Brinker's. A match flickered. "Nine o'clock," the agency clerk announced. "It'll be dark outside."

A weary wait and then it was ten. The hour made Dave think of ten in the morning when they'd drop Grady through a trap. And of a girl in town who was counting each relentless minute! A new surge of impatient anger came to Harbison. "Look, Jake. Maybe someone at Sunderlin's'll take a ride into Salmon tonight. He'll tell about your telegram."

Jake, who wore a fleece-lined jacket, had fallen asleep. The answer came from Brinker. "If it was Saturday night there'd be a fair chance of it. But it's Wednesday. I didn't see anyone at Sunderlin's who'd likely be going in the middle of the week. All the loafers in the county are already there. They went in to see the hanging."

"Bunch up or we'll freeze," Mitchell shivered. He slid along the wall till his shoulder touched Dave's.

Through another weary wait there was no sound except deep breathing from the stage driver. Then Dave heard the snort of a frightened horse. Instantly he was alert. "Might be Smiley. Maybe he sobered up and came home."

But shouts drew no response. "Likely that horse smelled a bear," Mitchell said. "Or heard a panther. What time is it, Fred?"

"This is my last match." When it flared Brinker gave the time. "Straight up midnight, Mitch."

That same midnight, thirty miles away, a girl stood at her hotel room window. An untouched bed showed she'd had no sleep. A haggard despair pinched her small delicate face and her eyes, long past crying, were mirrors of stark terror. The thing she tried not to look at kept rising in front of her; even with her eyes shut she could see it; if she ever slept again she would dream it, and hate it, and feel forever the force of its brutal taunt.

For it was a lie! She knew her father couldn't possibly have done that thing. He was kind, decent, gentle; since her childhood, except for these last few years at a boarding school, he'd been father and mother to her. And so that ugly tower of white pine, over there in the jailyard, stood up like a ghastly, taunting lie in the starlight.

Beam by beam she'd watched it grow, this last week, until yesterday's news sheet had described its completion — giving details as though it were some new bandstand in the park. ". . . Nineteen feet high," the cold print said, "with a drop of eight feet. The frame is twenty by twenty, with stairs leading up to it from the yard."

In just ten hours they'd be taking Court Grady to that scaffold. Lisa Grady could see every gaunt angle of it through a gap of space between the express office and Colonel Shoup's store. Except for three lighted saloons

Main Street was dark. The saloons were full right now; so were this hotel and both the town's rooming houses. A legal hanging was a rare event and to see this one the morbid had flocked in from all corners of the range.

A lamplit window across from Pope's saloon marked the sheriff's office. It went dark and Lisa saw the spare, stooped frame of Ad Gilroy emerge on the walk. He lived here at the International Hotel in a room only a few doors down the hall. When he headed this way the girl knew he was coming home for the night.

In a last pitch of desperation she went out into the hall and waited in front of his door. It wouldn't do any good but she couldn't resist making one more appeal. He was a stern, stubborn man, but just and reasonably sympathetic. Every day since her arrival before the trial he'd let her talk with her father through cell bars. Patiently he'd answered all her questions and had shown her all reports on the case.

As she waited at his room door she could hear talk from the bar and lobby below. A clink of glasses carried eerily to Lisa. "Does Grady still claim that alibi witness, Ed? I mean that stranger he dreamed up?"

"He's standing pat on it, Gus." The voice was proprietor Ed Edwards' who, after gleaning a fortune from the Leesburg diggings, had moved into Salmon City to build what he called the finest hotel in central Idaho.

"He's bound to have done it," Gus insisted. "Old Dan and Annie Richmire ain't the kind who'd lie a man's life away."

Lisa herself was sure of that much. She'd gone out to see the Richmires and was convinced of their sincerity. It simply meant they were mistaken. They must have seen someone other than Court Grady.

The girl heard Sheriff Gilroy come in from the street. Talk stopped as he crossed the lobby. Yet the very abruptness of the silence mirrored their thought: that here was a tired old man on his way to get a little sleep; a man who in just ten hours would become the second most important figure in a jailyard tragedy. For it was Sheriff Ad Gilroy who must escort the prisoner to his doom, adjust the noose with his own hands and give a signal for the drop.

Lisa heard that silence and her own wretched heartbeats measured every step as Gilroy crossed the lobby, mounted the stairs. Suddenly he loomed in the hallway's dimness, facing her. A man of years, with rounded shoulders and a drooping gray mustache, his look of tiredness deepening as he saw the girl waiting at his door.

He spoke gently. "I wish I could make it easier for you, Lisa. You know I can't. There ain't nothing I can do but my duty."

"Why didn't the stage come in?" she asked him.

He shrugged. "No tellin'. They must've called off the run, for one reason or another."

"It was the last chance for mail."

He knew what she meant; he'd seen her waiting by the post office at seven o'clock, when the Red Rock stage was due in. He knew she'd written many appeals to Governor Neil at Boise. "It just ain't any use, Lisa."

"But I didn't tell him about the four loaves," Lisa said, "till only a week ago. I didn't know about them till then. And he hasn't answered."

The sheriff nodded. He himself wasn't much impressed by this last desperate point the girl had raised.

"It takes time," she reminded him again, "to mix dough and let it rise and mold it into loaves and then bake it into bread. On a cool day it could take six or seven hours."

He sighed patiently. She'd been harassing him for a week about it, had in fact recruited half a dozen women to prove that the making of bread on a cool day, from the mixing of milk and yeast to the final oven-baked loaf, was an all-day job.

"Even if it takes six hours," Gilroy said, "there's still a four-hour leeway." For the killing had occurred at six in the morning, ten hours before the arrest of Grady at his place twenty miles down the Lemhi. "He could ride the twenty miles in four hours and spend the next six baking bread."

"No man would do that!" Lisa protested.

"He might," Gilroy argued, "if he wanted to convince folks he'd been at home all day."

As to the freshness of the bread there was no doubt. Searching the ranch both indoors and out, they'd poked into every possible hiding place. A deputy had stuck a knife into four loaves of bread, on a chance that a two-pound gold dust bag might be concealed in each loaf — a probing which proved the loaves to be warm, soft, fresh. "Please ask your wife, sir," Lisa had written Governor Neil, "how long it takes to make bread."

"I've got to turn in now, Lisa." Sheriff Gilroy went into his room and the girl moved wearily toward her own.

Another door opened and out of it came a sweet-faced woman in a night robe. She slipped an arm around Lisa. "Tonight's no time for you to be alone," she said gently. "If you're not going to bed, won't you let me sit up with you?"

"That's awfully good of you," Lisa said. "But I don't want anyone with me. Goodnight, Mrs. Kane."

"You make me feel old, dear. Please call me Laura, won't you? And knock on my door if you get too wretchedly lonesome." Impulsively Laura Kane kissed Lisa's cheek and then went back to her room.

Lisa entered her own and again stood at the street window. Laura Kane was the only real friend she'd made here. During and since the trial, they'd breakfasted together each morning. An attractive divorcée in her early thirties, Mrs. Kane had been warmly sympathetic. Lisa knew vaguely that she had inherited a mining property at Shoup, some forty miles down the Salmon River, and had come here to sell it for the first fair offer.

A sound of trotting horses came to Lisa as a vehicle rolled into town. No ranch rig would be coming in at this hour and the girl took a feeble hope. It might be the stage from Red Rock, six hours late.

But it was only a buckboard full of young people returning from a frolic at some upvalley ranch. As their chatter floated to Lisa's window it seemed callous and even cruel in its impact on her own mood of despair. She saw the buckboard stop at Kingsbury's livery barn. The three homing couples got out there, then moved arm in arm down the walk till the dark swallowed them.

Again the street was quiet, dark except for the saloon lights. Yet the feeble hope still remained that last evening's stage had been delayed, and might yet arrive with mail. So Lisa Grady kept at her window, standing watch for it. To her left a wall of mountains reared like a black, jagged card. Whatever word good or bad came from the outside world, it would have to cross those mountains. They made a grim, rock-bound curtain, fencing off this valley, and to Lisa their very name seemed ominous. The Bitterroots! Bitterly and fearfully she looked at them, while minutes dragged into hours.

She was still there when the first glimmer of an early summer dawn touched the sky, above and beyond the blackness of that bleak, eastern divide.

CHAPTER
THREE

The same flush of dawn found a man named Smiley riding a mule toward his cabin home, up a narrow side gulch from the Agency Creek stage road. Ten hours of hard drinking followed by twenty hours of sodden sleep had left his face bloated and his stomach sick. His head was too big and his throat was stuffed with dry cotton. The only cure for it was on his cabin shelf.

He'd wakened with a terrible thirst for which he'd gulped a quart of water from his washstand pitcher. Next he'd needed a slug of whisky; but at five a.m. the bar at Sunderlin's was closed. The only way to get that slug — and getting it fast was a desperate must — was to make tracks to his gulch cabin.

As he reined up in front of it, he blinked at what was surely a delusion born of his debauch. An empty stagecoach! Smiley's puffy eyes stared, knowing it couldn't be real. This was a dead end gulch and no one in his right mind would drive a stage up it.

Then Smiley saw horses; four stage horses unfed since noon yesterday and stamping rebelliously in the cabin's corral. One of them whinnied a complaint. Immediately Smiley heard voices and a pounding on wood. It seemed to come from the dugout cellar.

"That you, Smiley? Let us outa here!"

Smiley dismounted, tried to shake the fuzziness from his brain. Light was a bit brighter now and he saw a padlock in the hasp of the dugout door. Since nothing was there worth stealing, he'd left it unlocked.

Again he heard shouting. Smiley fumbled for a key and with it unsnapped the padlock. As he raised the sloping door five disheveled men staggered up the steps. Smiley recognized a stage driver. All of them were stiff from huddling overnight in a cold damp hole.

The youngest and briskest of them was a man Smiley had never seen before. He had a yellow envelope and with it he headed straight to Smiley's saddled mule.

"We're borrowin' it," Jake Slavin announced tersely. "Mitch, you and Brinker help me hitch up the stage. Harbison, when you get to Jeb Carter's place five miles below here, get yourself a fresh mount. Do the same at Tendoy and Baker. Wait a minute; I'd better give you a note."

Slavin scribbled on a scrap of paper.

Bearer carries a telegram from the governor. It's to stop a hanging. Give him a fresh horse.

Jake Slavin.

It was all too fast for Smiley. He stood gawking as the young man they called Harbison — the only one who wasn't too weak and stiff to tackle a hard, forced ride — took the note and spurred off down the gulch.

The first leg of Dave's ride was the slowest. The mule had to be bullied into a run and it was an hour before

Dave rode him into the barnyard of a small trailside ranch. He was out of the timber now, on the edge of the wide Lemhi Valley. Jeb Carter was heading for his barn with a milk pail when Dave hailed him.

"Read this!" He showed Slavin's note and flashed the telegram.

"Shoot me fer a Sheepeater Injun!" The rancher thumbed toward his corral. "Help yourself. That piebald bay's the fastest. You can leave him at Tendoy."

In a few minutes Dave was on his way again. Pounding on toward Tendoy he looked back and saw Jake's stagecoach emerging from the Agency Creek timber. Those unfed horses were dragging at a walk; but Jake would get fresh ones at Tendoy.

They'd figured it all out, waiting in the dark dugout. Jake would stick with his coach and Harbison, youngest and strongest of five men, would make the dash to town.

Dave loped the bay a mile, walked a half mile, then spurred to a lope again. Behind him the sun had just topped the Bitterroots and ahead, centering this broad, grassy valley, a line of willows marked Lemhi Creek. A cluster of log shacks showed the spot where Agency Creek joined the Lemhi. The Tendoy stage station.

At three minutes before seven Dave pulled up there, his mount lathered and blowing. His yell brought the station master and Dave showed him Jake's note. The man swore under his breath as he led Dave to the corral. "Damn those wranglers of mine! They took both my saddle mounts and rode in to see the hangin'. You'll have to ride a stage horse, I reckon."

He picked a gaunt buckskin which was broken to both harness and saddle. While the man saddled the animal, Dave gulped a cup of coffee. Then he was off, racing down the Lemhi. This harness horse was awkward, roughgaited; it had only two gaits; a walk and a jolting trot. After each walk it was harder to spur the brute into a trot again. Time was burning and Dave thought of a girl in the town ahead; a girl waiting in dread for the hour of ten. He dug in with his spurs. "Step along, damn you! We got a deadline!"

A ranch halfway to the next station was deserted. Its people, Dave guessed, had gone in to attend the hanging. But the corral had a calico pony and Dave remembered instructions from Jake. "Don't stand on ceremony, boy. Grab any bronc in sight and keep goin'. I'll square it later."

Dave saddled the calico, found it willing but too shortlegged for speed. He pressed on, fording the Lemhi twice in the next three miles. At the next fording he let the calico drink sparingly. An odd name, Lemhi! Then he remembered reading about a colony of Mormons who in 1854 had settled briefly in this valley, naming it for some king in their Book of Mormon.

The calico began blowing and Dave pampered it for a mile. Ahead, a mountain skyline beyond the Salmon River drew slowly nearer. His watch lacked a hundred minutes of ten o'clock and the town was still fifteen miles away. Dave leaned forward, pressed with his knees and coaxed the pony to a canter. In the distance he saw a group of sheds which was sure to be the Baker relay station, last stage stop on the Red Rock to Salmon

City run. "It's as far as you go, Patch. What about a stretch pace? Okay?"

The pony gave its best and was running at a lope when the eastbound stage, which had left town at seven, met and passed them. Its driver waved a hand. "Better hurry, cowboy, or you'll miss the show." He rattled on toward Tendoy in a cloud of dust.

Fifteen minutes later Dave reined up at Baker and found only the station master's wife there. She was a rugged, raw-boned woman. "Every man on the place lit out for town," she told Dave, "quick as they changed teams a while ago. It's heathenish, I say, wantin' to see somebody hanged."

Dave showed her Jake's note and she erupted into action. "Take the roan mare. I'll saddle up myself and ride as far as Mulkey's with you, in case nobody's there."

She was stirrup to stirrup with him as Dave raced on down the valley. It was only five miles to Mulkey's and these were strong, grained horses. "We can lope every foot of it." The Baker woman sat astride a stock saddle, her skirt bunched above her knees, flipping her quirt from flank to flank.

Two miles beyond Baker she pointed to a log house on the bank of the Lemhi. It had a meadow of native grass. "That's the Court Grady place. He's been a good neighbor and I never did think he did it."

"We've got just seventy minutes," Dave muttered, "to save his neck."

They spurred on, splashing across a small tributary creek coming down from the Bitterroots. "Geerston

Crik," the woman said; and vaguely Dave recalled mention of it by Mitchell. Something about a bear hunt up Geerston.

"Everybody at Mulkey's'll be in town," the Baker woman said, "unless it's Alcinda herself. Alcinda's got a thoroughbred with a singlefoot gait. Eats up the road. It can make the seven miles to town in thirty minutes."

The roofs of a large ranch loomed ahead. It had a long alfalfa meadow skirting the creek. "Biggest layout in the valley," the Baker woman said, "except for Marvin Kane's place up at Junction. Eli Mulkey came out in '66 and struck it rich over the hill at Leesburg. Then he slapped his stake into land and cattle."

They turned into a hedged lane and rode to a ranchyard. With dismay Dave saw no sign of life. At the house every blind was drawn and every door locked. Not only the crew, but Alcinda Mulkey herself had gone to town.

"But she drove in," the Baker woman exclaimed. "There's that saddle horse of hers." In a paddock Dave saw a long-limbed chestnut.

The woman from Baker uncoiled a rope and Dave opened the paddock gate. It took only a minute to rope and saddle the chestnut; and as long again to get out to the main road.

Dave took off down it at a lope and after a hundred yards the horse broke into an easy, rhythmic singlefoot. It was a beautiful gait. Looking back Dave saw the Baker woman waving her hat. "Don't stop for nothin'!" she yelled. Dave blessed her and rode on.

His watch said nine-thirty-three. "Means you got to break your own record. You heard what the lady said; we don't stop for nothin'."

It was poetry, the movement of that horse. The hooves flashed, clopping the trail with the precision of drumbeats. The rushing riffles of the Lemhi kept pace with them, leaping onward to join a broader, deeper river at the town.

Another mile and Dave could see roofs of the taller stores and the green of box elder lining a street. Nine-fifty! In just ten minutes they'd be springing the trap. Dave fought back an urge to use spurs. A spurring might break this steady, mile-eating gait.

The last mile seemed endless and the nip-and-tuck suspense brought cold sweat to Dave Harbison. Ever since the holdup of the stage some inner sense had told him that Court Grady wasn't guilty. The holdup itself proved an evil influence afoot, some sinister guilt or purpose which needed to checkmate Grady's reprieve and get him out of the way. Nor would the governor have issued the stay without reason.

Dave jumped the chestnut over an irrigation ditch and wheeled into the town's main street. Ranch rigs and saddle horses lined it. A crowd jammed it, overflowing it from walk to walk, a silent, expectant crowd like the audience of a play at curtain time.

It was ten o'clock, straight up, with everyone waiting there, breathless, counting the final seconds of a life. All of Lemhi County, from the Bitterroots to the Yellowjacket Mountains, had flocked in for this Roman holiday. They all faced toward a common focus, a tower of pine planking in the jailyard. At the edge of the crowd Dave hit the ground, dropped the reins and began pushing savagely through. Over their heads he saw three men at the foot of steps leading up to the trap platform. One of them, a priest, crossed himself and turned away. The other two, one with a sheriff's badge and the other wristbound, moved slowly up the steps.

Dave shouted to them. He plunged through the crowd and got to the jailyard. "A telegram from the governor, Sheriff!" His voice shocked the stillness. The sheriff stared down at him as Dave waved his yellow envelope.

A thousand startled eyes saw him scamper up the steps. A noose dangled there, ready to be looped around a man's neck. "For you, Sheriff!" Dave announced as he appeared beside the two up there. He handed over the sealed telegram. "A man held up Slavin's stage; that's why you didn't get it last night."

The sheriff gaped. Then he broke the envelope and read the message. A haggard relief showed on his face as he spoke to the prisoner. "Looks like that gal of yours turned up somethin', Grady."

He looked down at the crowd and yelled hoarsely: "Go on home, everybody. Governor Neil wired a thirty-day stay."

Grady had been standing with his chin level, braced for his fate. Now the sudden letdown sapped him and his knees buckled. Dave Harbison caught him as he collapsed in a faint.

CHAPTER
FOUR

A moment more of spine-prickling stillness down there. Then a roar from the street. Men who'd watched morbidly for death now cheered raucously for life. Above the noise the sheriff made himself heard to Dave. "There's a girl named Lisa at the hotel. Get over there fast and show her this, while I put him back in his cell."

He gave Dave the telegram and took the limp Grady in his arms.

Dave scooted down the steps. A hundred men swarmed about him with questions. He fought his way past them and toward a sign, "International Hotel," which marked a building at the next corner. Getting clear of the crowd Dave made for it at a run.

It was a two-story frame with a railinged porch on the Main Street side. Dave dashed in and found the lobby deserted. The desk clerk was out in the street crowd. Dave looked to the right into an empty dining room and to the left into a bar. The barroom was deserted except for a small, goateed Chinese bartender. "I'm looking for Lisa Grady."

"Lady in parlor." The midget bartender wore a starched white apron. "Come, I show you."

He led Dave down a hallway to a carpeted sitting room. Two women, one a dozen years older than the other, were seated on a sofa there. By her pale, tragic face Dave knew that the younger one was Lisa Grady. She sat stiffly upright with clenched hands, waiting for the end of her long, hopeless death watch. The older woman had an arm around her.

"I have good news, Miss Grady. Read it yourself." Dave advanced with the open telegram.

The girl looked at him dumbly. Her dark hurt eyes had the deadness of despair. "It's too late!" she murmured. The parlor clock said ten-fifteen.

"It's *not* too late," Dave said gently. "A close call, but I got here on time with it."

The older woman took the telegram and read it. "It's true!" she confirmed joyously. "We've got thirty days, Lisa!" She gave the girl a hug.

Lisa herself read the message, then burst into tears with her face pressed in a hysteria of relief against the older woman's shoulder.

It was the little Chinese bartender who knew just what to do. "You like go to him, yes, Miss Lisa?" Grotesquely gallant in his ankle-length apron, he stepped forward and offered his arm.

"Thank you, Chung. Yes, please take me to him."

By the time Dave Harbison realized he should have made the offer himself, Chung and Lisa Grady were leaving the parlor with quick steps, on the way to a cell at the jail.

The other woman looked after them with a nod of understanding. "Chung likes her and she trusts him.

He used to be a cook and it was he who reminded her of the time it takes to make bread. She wrote the governor about it. Is that why he sent the reprieve?"

"I don't know," Dave said with a wry smile. "All I know is my stomach's about to cave in. Haven't had a bite since noon yesterday."

"You poor boy! I'm Laura Kane and I have a weakness for hungry boys. Let's go to the kitchen and see what we can find."

Passing through the lobby they found it still deserted. Everyone was in the street, milling around, besieging the sheriff's office to find out the why of Grady's reprieve.

Laura Kane led Dave through an empty dining room and into the hotel kitchen. "I was afraid of this," she said when she found the staff gone. "They're out in the crowd, I suppose. Will ham and eggs do? What about pancakes? Here's batter left over from breakfast."

The range had live coals and Dave put in some firewood. A coffee pot was half full. "While it's warming up, I better go wash."

When he came back from the washroom Laura Kane had ham sizzling in one pan and was scrambling eggs in another. "How many pancakes?" she asked.

"About forty'll do for a start."

Presently she served him at the kitchen table, sitting opposite with a cup of coffee. "Now tell me, please. Where did you get the telegram?"

While he told her about the holdup Dave became aware of an oddly puzzled look growing in her eyes; a look curious and personal, as though she were probing Dave himself rather than his story.

Then people began coming in. A cook, a dishwasher, a waitress. From the lobby came voices as clerk and guests returned from the excitement outside. "The only way we can figure it," Dave finished, "is that the masked guy knew about the reprieve and didn't want it delivered. If you want to know who he is and why, your guess is as good as mine."

And still Laura Kane's eyes kept searching him with a growing personal interest. "You remind me of someone," she said. "It's something about your curly brown hair and the shape of your head. You haven't told me your name yet."

"I'm Dave Harbison."

"Of course!" The woman's eyes widened. "You *do* look like him. A Gregg Harbison I knew once. He left this range — let's see — it was four years ago."

"He was my brother."

"Your brother? But you're too young . . ."

"I'm twenty-two. Gregg was twelve years older. I was a kid in school when he went west. You say you knew him?"

"Quite well. He was a cowboy on my husband's ranch, up the Lemhi. But only for a season. He left us and went to southern Idaho."

Dave's face took on a grimness. "You heard what happened to him?"

She nodded. "It was in the papers. We were all shocked by it. Everyone liked Gregg Harbison."

36

"*Someone* didn't!" Dave corrected bitterly. "Someone shot him in the back from a patch of willows."

"And they never found out who did it?"

"No. That's why I came west, soon as I turned twenty-one. To find out who did it!"

Her searching eyes asked, If you find out, what will you do about it? Was this a crusade of vengeance? But Laura Kane didn't put it into words.

A rumble of wheels was followed by a noisy entrance at the front. Then the lobby clerk came to the kitchen with a message for the cook. "It's Jake Slavin's stage with three passengers. They're sixteen hours late and half starved. Dish up some grub for 'em."

The cook and his helpers got busy. Dave heard four men troop into the dining room — men who'd shared a dugout with him last night.

Laura Kane replenished his plate. "But it was two years ago," she said, "and it happened a long way from here." Hailey was some two hundred miles to the southward.

"I went to the Hailey diggings," Dave told her, "and poked around nearly a year there. Couldn't turn up a thing. They say nobody down that way had it in for Gregg. He wasn't robbed. All the guy did was sneak up and shoot him in the back. But there was bound to be a reason; so I decided to backtrack over his life."

Mrs. Kane refilled his coffee cup. Presently he leaned back and rolled a cigarette. "I learned that before taking up mining in the Hailey district, he'd put in a few months on a stage-driving job south out of Boise. So I went there and asked at every relay station he'd ever changed teams at. They remembered Gregg, but said he'd never had a run-in with anybody. He'd come there, they said, from a ranch job up in Lemhi County. So here I am."

"You'll find the same thing here," Laura Kane predicted. "I'm sure your brother never quarreled with anyone at the ranch."

"Why did he quit and go south?"

"He never told us."

Dave nodded moodily. He'd been west long enough to know the code. Cowboys everywhere came and went, usually with no questions asked or answered.

Questions, by the volley, were being asked and answered in the dining room. Dave could hear the sheriff firing them at Jake Slavin. "He had a black, brushy beard," Jake was telling him. The voice of Brinker chimed in: "He was about your build, Sheriff. Had on a brown corduroy coat and rode a brown horse."

The word "horse" brought Dave to his feet. "I clean forgot mine! That singlefooter I borrowed at Mulkey's! Left him standin' in the middle of the street. Thanks, Mrs. Kane. I better go round him up."

He was crossing the dining room when Slavin stopped him. "That's him, Sheriff. Hi, Harbison. You sure burned up the road. We were a lap behind you all the way in."

"Wait till I take care of my horse," Dave said.

"No rush about it," the sheriff said. "You must be plenty saddle-weary after that ride. Better take a room and get some sleep."

"I'll do that, Sheriff." Dave passed through the lobby where he picked up his hat. He went out to find the street still crowded. A hundred pair of eyes recognized him as the fast-riding messenger who'd stopped a hanging.

A grizzled rancher slapped his back. "You look like you need a drink, young fella. Come have one on me."

"Some other time," Dave said. He spotted the chestnut singlefooter at a rack in the next block. When he got to it he found a man in a long, clerical coat standing by. "Looks like you're right popular," the man grinned. "All the world loves a lifesaver, I guess. I saw your mount in the street and tied him here. My name's Booth. I publish the *Weekly Recorder*."

"Which is the best livery barn, Mr. Booth?"

"All three are okay. Nearest is Kingsbury's. I'll walk along with you."

As Dave led the chestnut half a block to a stable, Editor Booth kept at his elbow with brisk questions. He was a skilful reporter and quickly drew out most of what Dave had told Laura Kane.

"So you're Gregg Harbison's kid brother!" Booth was keenly interested, for the story was double-barreled now. This curly-haired young stranger, having come to Idaho to check on one unsolved murder, had run bang into another.

"Mrs. Kane says he rode for her husband's ranch, four years ago."

Booth nodded. "Marvin Kane's Kaybar outfit. That was before Laura went to California and got a divorce. Marv took to drinking too much and she left him."

"How long has she been back here?"

"Only a month or so. An uncle of hers down at Shoup left her a mine and she's trying to sell it." The *Recorder* man lighted a stogie and puffed it comfortably. "Marv Kane's setting up to her again. He quit drinking after she left him. Wants her back but she won't have anything to do with him."

After stabling the horse they went out to the street. "How big was the Kaybar four years ago, when my brother worked there?"

"Eight or ten riders, maybe. But I never heard of any of 'em having a grudge against Gregg Harbison."

"Any of those eight or ten riders still work there?"

"I don't know. Why don't you ask Kane himself? He's over at Pope's bar right now with some of his hands. I've got time to point him out, if you like."

Dave went with him to Pope's saloon and found every inch of the bar space taken. Again he was recognized as the rider who'd raced into town on Alcinda Mulkey's horse. "Dagged if it ain't Mr. Paul Revere hisself!" exclaimed the bartender. "Step up, mister, and hoist one on the house."

Booth steered Dave past them and found Marvin Kane playing cards with three of his hands. All four were rugged and gunslung. The rancher himself had a well-featured, saddle-colored face shaded by a tall stockman's hat. He stood up to shake hands when Booth presented Dave.

He listened to Dave's question and gave a prompt nod. "Sure I remember Gregg. He mentioned a kid brother back in Missouri. Gregg was a top hand and we

40

hated to see him go. It was right after the fall roundup, four years ago."

"Any of that outfit still riding for you?"

"Only Wes Gordon here." Kane thumbed toward the stockiest of his companions. Dave noticed a bullet scar on the man's broad, swarthy forehead. "I carried a nine-man payroll that season, but except for Wes they've all drifted on."

"Any of 'em ever get sore at Gregg? Enough to build up a grudge and keep riding it?"

Kane smiled and shook his head. "Not even Wes here." He winked at the other two riders. "Even if Gregg *did* beat him out in the roping contest, at the county fair that year."

"Thanks. I won't keep you." Dave went out with the *Recorder* man.

"I just remembered," Booth said. "At that same county fair there was a gunplay in Pinky Ogle's poker dive down by the river. A man was caught cheating and had to shoot his way out. He killed a dealer and no one ever saw him again."

"Yeh? What's that got to do with my brother?"

"There were six witnesses. Seems to me one of them was a Kaybar man. Might've been Gregg Harbison. We can ask Pinky Ogle."

"Take me to him, please."

They walked to the foot of Main Street where a timber bridge spanned the Salmon River. The current was wide and swift. A flat-bottom boat was tied at a wharf and crates were being loaded on it. Surprise at seeing a boat on such turbulent water showed on

Dave's face and brought a smile to Booth's. "The boats only go one way," he explained. "They shoot 'em downriver to Shoup, then dismantle 'em to use the lumber for cabins there. The boat crews come back by trail."

Shoup, Dave remembered, was where Laura Kane had a mine. He followed Booth into a tawdry riverbank saloon. The place had a sawdust floor with card and dice tables. The man who owned it was practicing card tricks. "Pinky," Booth asked him, "can you remember the names of those six witnesses at the gunplay here four years ago, during the county fair?"

The only pink thing about Pinky was a long oval birthmark under his left ear. His eyes and his hair were as black as the stubble on his chin. He squinted the eyes and thought back. "Sure thing, Mr. Booth." He rattled off six names and one of them was Gregg Harbison.

"Thanks." Booth and Dave left the place and walked back up Main. "There's your motive," the editor suggested. "Maybe two years after Gregg left here the killer turned up at the Hailey diggings. Maybe your brother recognized him."

It was possible, Dave admitted. "I'll sleep on it, Mr. Booth. And much obliged."

Booth turned in at his printing shop and Dave went on to the hotel. As he registered there a hush of deference came over the lobby. The desk clerk was almost obsequious. "The stage driver brought your bag in, Mr. Harbison. I put it in number ten. Fifth door on the right, down the hall."

He handed over the key and Dave started down the ground floor hall. As he passed the hotel parlor a girl appeared in its doorway. A slight, dark-eyed girl with all the tears gone and a face radiant with hope and gratitude.

"I've been waiting to thank you," she said.

The way Lisa Grady thanked him took the breath from Dave. She stood on tiptoes and kissed his lips. Then she slipped by him. Before Dave came out of his shock she was running up the stairs to her room.

CHAPTER
FIVE

The kiss was still tingling on his lips when Dave dropped into sleep. At sundown the clerk's knock wakened him, calling him to supper. He took a fresh shirt from his bag, then brought out a forty-five gun. After debating a moment he put the gun under the pillow of his bed. A mirror reminded him he hadn't shaved since Red Rock. He took time for it now, brushing his hair and boots. Maybe he'd see Lisa Grady in the dining room.

On the way there he glanced into the hotel bar and saw the cattle buyer Whipple drinking with a short, broad man with a holstered gun on his leg. Whipple beckoned. "Join us, Harbison?"

It made the other man turn his head and Dave saw that he was Wes Gordon of the Kaybar. The fact made Dave join them and accept a short beer.

"I'm trying to nail down dates, Gordon. Do you remember just what month my brother joined the outfit, and just when he quit?"

"He joined us in the spring," Gordon said, "and stayed on through the fall pick-up. April through October, I'd say."

"Thanks. And much obliged for the beer." Dave left them and crossed to the dining room.

One of the diners was Sheriff Gilroy. He called Dave to his table. "Didn't want to wake you up, boy, after that hellbender ride of yours. So I been waitin' for you here. Maybe you'll remember somethin' Jake Slavin overlooked."

A waitress took Dave's order. While she was bringing it he described the holdup at a creek crossing below Sunderlin's relay station.

The sheriff made a few notes, comparing them with what he'd jotted down while talking to Slavin. "You tell it just like Jake did. But that assayer Mitchell says the guy had on a brown corduroy coat and baggy pants."

"Mitchell's right," Dave said. "And now that you mention it, I remember something else. Those baggy knees had gray stains on 'em."

"You mean sand stains? Like a man gets when he kneels by a creek to pan gravel?"

"No, they were powdery stains, more like fresh gray ashes, like he'd just kneeled by a campfire."

"Humph!" Gilroy rubbed his chin thoughtfully. "Jake says he saw camp smoke in the woods across the creek from Sunderlin's. I sent a deputy up there to check. But if Baggy Knees was camping in the woods, he'll be a long way off by now."

"All we can bet on," Dave said, "is that he didn't want that reprieve delivered."

"Which means he wanted Grady dead. But why?"

Dave mentioned the vague and sketchy theory he'd suggested in the dugout: "Maybe Grady knows

45

something he doesn't know he knows; but if he lives long enough it might pop back into his mind."

The sheriff wasn't impressed. He was a hard fact man. His eyes followed Dave's across the room. "She fed me in the kitchen," Dave murmured. "Who's that with her?"

"You mean with Laura Kane? He's Matt Garside, a broker she listed her Shoup mine with." A knowing smile lighted Gilroy's face. "So far the only luck he's had is an excuse to eat with her every night, so he can report on what progress he's makin'. Fact is the only progress he wants to make is with Laura herself. He knows that if he sells that mine for her she'll head straight back to California."

Dave looked about for Lisa Grady but she wasn't here. Two of his recent stage-mates, Mitchell and Brinker, were eating together. And Marvin Kane, he noted, was sharing a table with the *Recorder* man, Booth. Booth was gesturing covertly toward Dave and the sheriff, which meant he was discussing the day's sensation. But the cattleman seemed not to hear him; his eyes were fixed wistfully on his ex-wife, Laura. It made Dave remember what Booth had said about Kane wanting her back.

"Does Booth keep a file of his old papers?" Dave asked.

"You want to read up on the Grady case?"

"Not right now, Sheriff; but I'd like to browse through the issues for four years ago; say from April through October."

"We'll ask Booth if he's got 'em," Gilroy said.

★ ★ ★

46

After supper they waited in the lobby till Booth and Kane came out. The cattleman stopped at the cigar counter and Dave asked Booth about the news files.

The editor nodded. "Come along and I'll show you," he invited.

Dave went with him to the printing office. There Booth lighted a lamp and led the way into a musty storeroom at the back. In a closet was the paper's morgue, the back issues bound under pasteboard cover in surprisingly neat order. "Which ones do you want?"

"The ones from April to October, four years ago," Dave said.

"Better take the entire 1878 file." When Booth lifted it from its niche it wasn't very thick or heavy, since the *Recorder* was only a four-page weekly. "When do you want to poke through them?"

"I'll start right now, if it's okay."

The editor looked about his storeroom and grimaced. "It's a dark, dusty hole here. Tell you what. If you'll guarantee to fetch it back, you can take this file to your hotel room for a few days. You'd have a cushioned chair there, and better reading light."

"Thanks a lot." Dave put the unwieldy volume under his arm and they went out to the street.

As they moved toward the hotel the editor looked at his watch. "We've got about five minutes," he remarked matter-of-factly.

It puzzled Dave. He'd lost track of time. Then he saw a score of people on the hotel's front walk. They were the town's top citizens and Booth introduced. Dave to a few of them. "This is our postmaster, Luther Marsh.

47

And this is Judge Corry; and our county attorney, Tom Copeland. You know Sheriff Gilroy, of course. And this is Colonel Shoup who'll be governor of Idaho some day; right now he runs the biggest store in Salmon and the biggest mine at Shoup."

"There she comes!" someone shouted, and the others looked expectantly up the street. From the easterly distance Dave heard a rumble of wheels. Of course! It would be the daily stage from Red Rock, due at seven o'clock. His own stage, except for the holdup on Agency Creek, would have pulled in at this same hour yesterday.

"I'd better open the mail pouch," the postmaster said, "right here on the walk."

In a group beyond him Dave saw Laura Kane standing with an arm around Lisa Grady. A tension of suspense held them. All they had so far was a telegram; the official reprieve itself should be carried by this oncoming coach.

The coach rattled up and brakes rasped as it stopped at the hotel. The driver tossed down a mail pouch. "Here she is, Luth."

Luther Marsh kneeled on the board walk by it. A tight circle of onlookers hid him from Dave's sight. Presently his voice rang out. "Here she is, Judge. It's addressed jointly to you and the sheriff."

Dave looked at Lisa and saw her relax. A stout envelope bearing a red waxen seal was passed to the judge. With the sheriff at his elbow he read the enclosure aloud:

Certain points brought to my attention lead me to order the execution of Court Grady postponed for thirty days. This then is a thirty-day reprieve, given under my hand and seal, in the hope that the time will be used in intelligent search for further evidence bearing on Grady's innocence or guilt.

John B. Neil,
Governor, Idaho Territory

To be rid of an awkward burden Dave took the file of papers to his room and tossed it on the bed. The room was hot and stuffy, so he opened a window. It was a north window giving to the hotel's hitch lot. Then he went back to the front sidewalk hoping to see Lisa; but both she and Mrs. Kane had disappeared.

So had Booth and the county officers. Those left on the walk closed in on Dave with questions. One of them was a rider from Alcinda Mulkey's ranch. Dave thanked him for the use of the chestnut singlefooter. "Tell your boss I never would've made it in time, with any ordinary horse."

"I'll take him back home tomorrow," the Mulkey hand grinned. "I'm Rufe Barrow. Buy you a drink?"

"Not tonight, thank you. See you again, Barrow."

Dave's muscles were still stiff from a night in the dugout. So he went back to room ten and made himself comfortable.

After kicking off his boots he drew a chair to the lamp and opened the 1878 news file to the month of April. He must make a note of every item which might conceivably have touched the life of Gregg Harbison.

49

Ninety per cent of the printed matter was made up of advertisements and plate copy which had nothing to do with local affairs. Page two always had an editorial; and page three a gossip column under the heading: "Lemhi County Briefs." Hardly anything else needed to be read.

An hour slipped by while Dave skimmed through the first three April issues. Then in the last April issue he saw his brother's name.

Marvin and Laura Kane drove in from the Kaybar Saturday for some spring shopping. Laura bought a new bonnet and Marvin a late model Winchester. He says his stock wintered well. One of his top riders, Art Pitkin, is quitting him. Sorry to see you go, Art. Marvin says he's replacing Art with a man from Missouri named Gregg Harbison. Welcome to Bitterroot Valley, Harbison.

Most of the local items were served up in the same intimate style. Dave copied this one in a notebook and marked it item 1.

He was on the second May issue when someone knocked at his door.

When he opened it he saw Pinky Ogle of the riverfront saloon. The man looked like he'd been in a fight. A blue-black bruise around his left eye certainly wasn't there at noon, when Dave and Editor Booth had called at his bar.

There was another difference. Ten hours ago this fellow had seemed in a reasonably pleasant mood. Now he looked sullen and angry. Angry, no doubt, at whoever had punched him in the eye. A man is likely to talk, Dave thought, when he's mad; so he invited this one in.

"What's on your mind, Ogle?"

Pinky Ogle slouched in and crossed to the open window. He leaned out of it to look cautiously both ways. The hitch lot was dark, quiet. Dave watched the man narrowly. Except for a pair of fancy riding boots, Pinky was shabbily dressed. He came back to the bed, sat on it, leaned furtively toward Dave and spoke from an edge of his mouth. "I hear talk at the bars, mister. They say you're lookin' for a killer."

"That's right; the one who sniped my brother down near Hailey."

Ogle lowered his tone to a hoarse whisper. "What's it worth if I put a name to him?"

"Plenty." But Dave was skeptical and wary. Maybe this fellow really knew something; but more likely he was just a cheap chiseler who'd come here to peddle some trumped-up tip.

"How much?" Pinky bargained.

"Depends," Dave sparred, "on whether I believe you or not. How would I know you're naming the right man?"

"*How did I get this?*" The words came spitting spitefully from Ogle as he touched his bruised eye. "Far as that goes, I got *proof,* mister."

And suddenly it made sense to Dave. The bruise was fresh and told at least part of its own story. "You went to someone else first, didn't you?" He took a firm grip on Pinky's wrist. "You offered to keep your mouth shut for a payoff. The only payoff you got was a poke in the eye. Made you mad so you came scooting to me."

"I got *proof!*" Pinky repeated. "Never mind how I got it. Ouch!" He wriggled to pull away.

Dave kept his grip. "How could you have proof? Were you down there when it happened?"

"Down at Hailey? No, I was right here in Salmon City. It was in May two years ago and I never left town all that month."

The date was correct. Gregg's body, several days dead, had been found in mid-May on the bank of a placer creek near Hailey, more than two hundred miles to the south. "If you weren't mixed up in it yourself, how could you know?"

Something sternly accusing in Dave's tone frightened Pinky. "I *don't* know!" he hedged. "I was just trying to shake you down."

"You wanted to shake me down, all right. But most of all you wanted to get even for that poke in the eye. Come along; I'm taking you to Sheriff Gilroy."

He'd need to put on his boots first. As Dave reached for them a gun boomed at his open window. Ogle screamed; he went down with his hands slapping to his chest.

Dave spun toward the window. Nothing was there but a smell of gunpowder and a black square of night. He heard a running retreat as the gunman sped alleyward across the hitch lot. Pinky Ogle, bleeding at the breast, lay dying on the floor and Dave remembered his own gun. He snatched it from under a pillow, leaped in his sock feet through the window and gave chase.

There was nothing to chase but sound. The lot had a few parked wagons, dim shapes in the starlight. Dave could still hear a running retreat and he tripped his trigger, sending a random bullet that way.

The bootsteps paused a moment as the runner turned to fire back. Dave saw the flash. The silhouette back of it was in a crouch that revealed nothing of height or figure. The man's bullet missed widely and crashed window glass back of Dave. Again he pulled his trigger with no real hope of a hit, shooting roughly toward a split-second flash.

The man ran a few strides farther, reached an alley back of a warehouse. There he turned and fired again. This time the bullet breathed on Dave and he felt a sting at his cheek. He raced on in pursuit, sock-footed. The tongue of a wagon tripped him and he sprawled headlong in the lot.

CHAPTER
SIX

Sheriff Ad Gilroy, at work in his Main Street office, heard the five shots and for a moment wasn't too much disturbed. The town was full of armed men and ever since the letdown at ten this morning, with Grady taken back to his cell, there'd been more than the usual amount of celebrating. Quite likely the shots came from someone blowing off steam.

Then Gilroy had a second thought and it sent him scurrying toward the hotel. The tone and order of the five shots struck him as significant. The tone told him that two guns had been in action; the order suggested alternate fire and return fire. The sheriff had a sensitive ear for gunfire. He knew that the depth of tone could be affected by the type of powder in a shell, the length of barrel or the calibre of bore.

At the hotel corner he saw people running into a dark hitch lot. Out of the lot's gloom came Dave Harbison. Dave in his sock feet with a forty-five six-gun in his hand. He was hatless, coatless, breathless and disheveled. "I lost him in the dark, Sheriff."

"Lost who?"

"Somebody shot Pinky Ogle. Here's one of his shells." The empty shell Dave gave to Gilroy was a forty-four.

"Shot Pinky where?" Gilroy demanded.

"In room number ten. You'll find him dead there. Come."

Gilroy followed Dave across the lot to the alley where the killer's retreat had last been heard. "He fired his last shot right about here. I picked up the shell. Didn't hear any horse, Sheriff. So he's likely still in town."

"He could be home in bed by this time," Gilroy growled.

"Or he could circle the block," Dave suggested, "and show up in some bar crowd."

Ogle, they found after checking at room ten, had died almost instantly. "I better scout the bars for a warm forty-four," Gilroy said. "Soon as you get your boots on, meet me at Pope's saloon."

As he pressed through a crowd in the lobby he snapped an order. "Round up the coroner, somebody."

A gun would soon cool and so Gilroy hurried on to Pope's bar. At least thirty men were there but only two of them had forty-fours. Both were clean and cool. Rushing on, Gilroy made the same test at the Bit Bar, with the same negative result. He was moving on toward the town's only fully equipped gambling club, Tony Sebastian's, when Dave Harbison caught up with him.

"The coroner showed up," Dave reported. "My room's a mess. They're moving me to another one."

"How much did you see of the killer?"

"Only his gun flash."

"Why did he do it?" They were walking briskly toward a brick building at the corner of St. Charles and

Main. Its ground floor was dark but its upper floor was brightly lighted.

"Ogle had a black eye. Claimed he had proof about who killed my brother. Right about then someone gunned him from the window."

It would be too late to check the warmness of a gun unless they hurried. Gilroy went quickly up the steps with Dave at his heels. At the top they burst into a suite of expensively furnished rooms offering roulette, faro, monte, poker and craps. The first room had a small, horseshoe-shaped bar with Tony Sebastian presiding. Tony's striped pants, winged collar and cutaway coat were impeccable, but his usual mellow mood was missing tonight. His face had a disgruntled look. "Anybody come in here," Gilroy demanded, "in the last twenty minutes?"

"Nobody but *them*." The gambler motioned toward two men at a table in the next room. They were matching coins for the drinks and neither of them was armed. Dave saw that they were Mitchell and Brinker who'd ridden the stage with him.

"I'm sure glad they put off that bear hunt," Mitchell was saying. "I'd be in no shape for it tomorrow."

Gilroy moved on through the suite of rooms with an eye for a forty-four gun. The only one he found was in the holster of a Kaybar rider, Wesley Gordon. The sheriff felt its barrel, smelled its breach, decided it hadn't been fired within the hour.

"What's goin' on?" Gordon demanded.

"That's what we're trying to find out," Gilroy snapped. "Who else is in town from your outfit, Gordon?"

"Only the boss. And he went to bed an hour ago."

Dave went on to the last room of the suite and found only two people in it. One was a glamorous redhead playing a piano and the other was a tall blond man with wavy hair parted in the middle. He was dressed like a well-to-do stockman, with belt and wristlets of filigreed leather. The forty-five in his holster had a mother-of-pearl grip. The girl wore an off-shoulder gown and Dave assumed she was the club's hostess. "Tony's as sour as a green crabapple, Cherry," the man was saying. "Whatsamatter with him?"

The girl laughed. They hadn't noticed Dave in the doorway. "Why wouldn't he be, Chuck?" With her fingers strumming the keys she purposefully struck a harsh discord. "After dropping five thousand at four-to-one odds. He thought he had a sure thing until . . ."

Her voice trailed off as she saw Dave there. For a moment she seemed embarrassed but quickly recovered. "Why, if it isn't the hero himself! Tony wasn't cross with you, I hope." She went to Dave with a cozy smile and put her hands on his shoulders. "You tipped over his cart, all right. But it'll teach him a lesson. He shouldn't give such long odds."

"Long odds on what?" The demand came from Sheriff Gilroy who appeared in the doorway beside Dave.

The girl's stare had surprise in it. "You mean you don't know? Isn't that why you're here?"

The blond young man looked at Gilroy with a teasing grin. "I'm afraid she overestimates you as a detective, Sheriff. She thinks you're checking up on Tony."

Gilroy looked impatiently from one to the other of them. "Why should I check up on Tony? If you know anything, Spoffard, let's have it."

The derisive grin widened on Spoffard's face. Cocksure conceit was there too, Dave thought. "All I know, Gilroy," the man jeered, "is that I was right when I told the voters they ought to make me sheriff, last election. Betcha they'll listen to me, this time. Cherry, since he's the only man in town who doesn't know about those odds Tony gave, you might as well tell him."

The redhead drooped her lips in a grimace. "Me and my big mouth! But I supposed everybody knew. Tony'll bet on anything if the odds are right. The weather; a roundup tally; or the time it takes to float a scow downriver to Shoup."

"Or a hanging!" Spoffard put in.

Gilroy gaped at them; and Dave felt the same shock of mixed surprise and disgust. He'd heard about inveterate gamblers betting on the turn of a card or on how long a man could stick on a bucking horse. But never on a hanging!

"It was like this," Cherry explained. "About a week ago one of our customers mentioned that Governor Neil might send a reprieve at the last minute. He did it in a southern county last year when they were about to hang a man named . . ."

She couldn't remember the name but Gilroy supplied it. "Sam Kidgeines. The reprieve went by stage from Boise to Hailey. Go on."

58

"So he might do it again, the customer said, in the case of Grady. 'Five 'll get you ten he don't,' Tony Sebastian said, and no one took him up. Later he offered three-to-one odds and still no one wanted the short end. Not with two eyewitnesses saying Grady did it."

"You mean no one put up any money?" Gilroy prodded.

"Not that night," Cherry said.

Chuck Spoffard gave the rest of it. "Couple of nights later when it began to look like a sure thing, Tony offered four-to-one odds on it. First one customer then another took him on. In all Tony had five thousand dollars riding on your noose, Sheriff. He stood to win a thousand if it came off on schedule — and to lose four thousand if it didn't."

"So you can't expect him to be very happy about it," Cherry said.

Gilroy whirled about and headed for the bar. And Dave, keeping pace, knew why. Here at last was a motive. A solid money motive. The Agency Creek holdup man could have been working for Sebastian. Tony was now five thousand dollars poorer because the attempt to stop delivery of the telegram hadn't succeeded.

At the bar Gilroy confronted Sebastian grimly. "Be at my office in twenty minutes," he commanded.

The gambler flushed. "What for? I haven't left here since supper."

"I'm not talking about Pinky Ogle. Twenty minutes! And don't be late. Come on, Harbison."

They went down to the street, Gilroy harassed and somber. "I'm shorthanded," he complained. "The only deputy I've got is Buck Blanchard; and I sent him to Sunderlin's. I need another one bad. What about lettin' me pin a badge on *you*?"

As they walked toward Pope's bar, Dave shook his head fretfully. "You'd put me on the wrong case, Sheriff. The Grady case. The one I want is the Gregg Harbison case and it didn't happen in your county."

"The Pinky Ogle case did," Gilroy countered. "And someone shut Ogle's mouth to keep him from talking about your brother. Work on any case you want, just so you do it with a county badge on. How about it?"

"I'll help out till your other deputy gets back," Dave agreed. "After that we'll see."

"Good!" Gilroy brought a brass badge from his pocket and pinned it on Dave's jacket. "Consider yourself sworn in. And don't forget this, boy. We've got three killings to work on: your brother's down south two years ago; Whitey Parks' up Lemhi Creek two months ago; and Pinky's tonight. Two of those three are tied together; might be the third one's linked in some way too."

To Dave the possibility seemed thin, almost incredibly remote, but he didn't argue the point. He followed Gilroy into Pope's bar and again they found some thirty customers.

The sheriff shouted for silence. "This is an order, men," he announced. "No sense in anyone gettin' sore about it. Unless he first gets my permission, nobody leaves town for thirty hours. There's a dead man at the

60

hotel and the killer is close by somewhere. Some time between noon and ten o'clock he blacked Pinky's eye."

There was a hubbub of protests, questions, suggestions. Only one of them carried weight. "I seen Pinky at sundown, Sheriff," a man said. "He didn't have any black eye then."

"That pinches down the time," Gilroy said. "Look, men. I've made Dave Harbison an emergency deputy. Spread the word. Help him all you can. If you hear about anyone beating up Pinky after sundown, bring it to my office. Let's go, Dave."

They moved on to the Bit saloon and made the same announcement. Here, where whiskies were two for a quarter, the patronage was a little shabbier. From there they went to the El Dorado.

"I'd better go meet Sebastian," Gilroy said. "Check the livery barns, Dave, and see if anyone's grabbed a horse. There comes Tony now."

The gambling man came up with a beet-red face. "Look, Gilroy; I got a dozen witnesses to prove I haven't left town for a week; or an inch from my bar since sundown."

"You've got more than that," Gilroy snapped back. "You've got a pal or two who'd cut a throat for five hundred dollars. Which is just a tenth of what you lost when Grady didn't swing today. Come along and let's talk about it." He hustled Sebastian toward his office with the gambler swearing bitterly every step of the way.

Dave took the opposite direction and stopped first at Kingsbury's barn. No one, the night man said, had called for his horse since the shooting. "If anyone tries to," Dave said, "tell him he'll have to get a clearance from Gilroy."

He left the same word at the other two livery stables. Then Dave saw a light in the printing shop and stopped in for a word with Booth.

The editor and his typesetter were busy in the press room. "We're getting out a special edition tomorrow, Harbison. About your race to town and the shooting of Ogle. I just saw Gilroy and he tells me you're a deputy."

"He's got Sebastian on the carpet?"

Booth nodded. "But he's not getting anywhere. It's a solid motive all right. Trouble is there's not a whisper of proof to back it up."

A stack of newly printed dodgers caught Dave's eye. SPOFFARD FOR SHERIFF was printed on them in tall letters. "What's this? Election stuff?"

"That's right. Chuck Spoffard ran for sheriff two years ago but Gilroy beat him out. Chuck figures to try again come November. Says he'll win this time. He'll plaster these posters all over the county."

"What are his chances?"

"Depends on whether Gilroy clears up these murders. There's the Grady case. And now Pinky's. And there's been a rash of gold dust robberies over in the Leesburg Basin. If Gilroy keeps flubbin' them, he'll get snowed under."

"He hasn't much time," Dave murmured. This was late in July, with election day less than four months away. "This Spoffard runs cattle, does he?"

"Yeh. He's got a ranch six or seven miles up the Salmon River. Runs about seven hundred head of grade Herefords."

"Any law enforcement experience?"

"Not that I ever heard of. Until a couple of years ago he rode for Marv Kane up at the Kaybar. By the way, have you seen Kane tonight?"

"Not since supper. His man Gordon says he went to bed early. Does he stay at the hotel?"

Booth shook his head. "When he was married he and Laura kept a town cottage up St. Charles Street. The Kaybar's too far out on the range for a round trip in one day. After Laura left him Marv kept on using the cottage to sleep in, whenever he's in town."

Dave yawned and stretched his arms. "Speaking of sleep, I can use some myself. See you tomorrow, Mr. Booth."

Walking to the hotel he pinned his mind on Spoffard. Only two years ago the man had been an ordinary hand at the Kaybar. Now he had a well-stocked ranch of his own. He'd need real money to start a spread like that. Where had it come from?

Had Spoffard worked for the Kaybar when Gregg was there? It was something to check on.

At the hotel Dave picked up the key to his new room. "It's number twenty-six on the second floor," the clerk said.

Dave heard voices from the bar and one of them had a familiar ring. He looked in and saw Chuck Spoffard. The tall, yellow-haired rancher was standing treat to a pair of miners. "Right under his nose!" Chuck was saying, "and he didn't even smell it. Hell of a sheriff he is!"

"Maybe after November we'll have a better one," a miner said. He raised his glass and they all drank to it.

It was clear to Dave that Spoffard was already hard at work electioneering. "Even now he wouldn't know about those bets of Tony's," the man chuckled, "if Cherry had kept her mouth shut. Not that I think Tony had anything to do with it. But it's a motive; and Gilroy muffed it a mile."

"I don't mind him muffing that one," a miner growled. "What riles me is the way he's been muffing those dust raids over in the basin. They're stealing us blind over there."

Dave advanced into the bar and appeared at Spoffard's elbow. "I just found out," he said quietly, "that you knew my brother Gregg."

Spoffard met his eyes and smiled affably. "Sure I did. Rode a season with him at the Kaybar." Then he noticed a badge on Dave's jacket. "So he pinned one on you! Can't say's I blame him. He sure needs help, that fella, the way he's been botchin' things up. Yeh, your brother and I rode for the same outfit. A swell guy, Gregg was. Bartender, slide out another glass. Name it, Harbison."

"No thanks," Dave said. "I'm on my way to bed. Got a busy day tomorrow."

"Readin' those four-year-old newspapers?"

"How did you know I had em?"

Spoffard grinned, shrugged his neatly tailored shoulders. "How could I help knowin'? The whole town's talkin' about what happened in your room tonight. That news file was open on your bed when the coroner dragged a dead man out of it." The grin broadened wisely. "Every barroom in town's been full of gab about it."

"About who punched Ogle in the eye and then shot him?"

"And they've even got a double slant on it," Spoffard confided. "One is that the guy shot Pinky to shut his mouth. The other is that he didn't expect to find Pinky there; he came to gun you down and then make off with that news file."

The idea hadn't occurred to Dave. "What's *your* slant on it, Spoffard?"

"It's none of my business right now," Spoffard quipped. "Ask me in November after they've elected me sheriff. You'll get quick action."

The man's brashness grated on Dave. But a quarrel with him would gain nothing; so with a curt goodnight Dave went up to his room.

It was a front corner room with a window facing Main and another looking down on the hitch lot. After lighting a lamp Dave saw his bag on a stand and Booth's news file on the bed.

He put them in a closet and undressed. It was a half hour after midnight when he crawled wearily under the blankets.

Sleep came at once and the awakening, two hours later, even more abruptly. A crash of glass was followed by a thud. A heavy object struck a wall of the room. Dave jumped out of bed and groped toward a window.

As he reached it a splinter of glass on the floor bloodied his bare foot.

From the window he could see only darkness. Both the street and the hitch lot were quiet and deserted. Dave limped to the lamp and lighted it. The light showed a smashed window pane. A half brick lay on the floor with a note tied to it. The note had nine scrawled words.

THE NEXT STAGE LEAVES AT SEVEN. BE ON IT.

CHAPTER
SEVEN

A half hour before stage time Dave Harbison went down to the lobby, wearing both a badge and a gun. The clerk gaped as he laid a brick-weighted note on the desk. "It's a visitor I had last night. Keep it for me while I eat breakfast."

Only a few guests were in the dining room. Dave brightened when he saw that one of them was Lisa Grady. She was alone at a wall table.

He stopped beside her. "Good morning. Mind if I join you?"

"Do." Her smile had a self-conscious restraint. "I hope you've forgiven me for being so . . . so emotional yesterday."

He knew she meant the impulsive kiss with which she'd thanked him. "It kept me going all day," he grinned.

A waitress took Dave's order. Then Lisa saw his deputy's badge and holstered gun. "You'll help Mr. Gilroy?" she asked hopefully.

"The best I can," he promised. "Do you know about last night?"

"I heard shooting. They say a man was shot in your room. Was there anything else?"

"Not much." He couldn't bear to tell her about the bets at Tony Sebastian's. To shift away from it he mentioned the tossed brick. "And we've got a man at Sunderlin's looking for a lead on that holdup."

"If we only knew *why!*" the girl sighed. "Have you any ideas at all, Mr. Harbison?"

"Back home the girls call me Dave. If you mean why did the man stop the stage, it was to delay the telegram. If you mean why did he want your father dead, I'm stumped." That was true because neither of the possibilities turned up so far satisfied Dave. If the real killer of Whitey Parks had inspired the holdup, there were many unanswered questions: such as how could he have known a reprieve would be on that particular stage; and how could he have known Smiley would be away from home sleeping off a spree. "We've got thirty days to find out," Dave said.

"We *must* find out!" Her face clouded. "If I could only do something!"

A thought hit Dave. "You can. You can do my home work while I ride a few trails. I mean I've got a lot of old newspapers to read. That's what I was doing when Ogle popped in. If you read 'em for me I could be doing something else."

He explained how he'd begun with the 1878 file, searching for any mentions of his brother Gregg or Gregg's connections.

"My father," Lisa Grady said, "didn't come out here till 1879."

"Okay. When you finish the '78 file, start on '79. Keep on reading right down to now. Copy any and all items that use either your dad's or my brother's name; or anything that might connect with them."

68

She leaned toward him, eagerly interested but confused. "How could that help us?"

"You never know," he brooded. "But people forget. And cold print doesn't. It tells tales and nails down dates. It couples names and places. All you'd have to read would be a column of local briefs on page three. It'd save me a lot of time."

"Of course I'll do it," the girl agreed. "And I'll get Laura Kane to help me."

A gruff voice intruded. "What's this?" Sheriff Gilroy stood by the table holding a half brick he'd picked up at the lobby desk.

Dave gave a shrug. "A bluff, maybe."

Gilroy looked again at the brick's message. Then he turned to scowl through a window at a stagecoach about to leave on its run to Red Rock. Driver Jake Slavin was inspecting his four harnessed horses. "It as good as says you'll be shot, boy, if you're not on it."

"Bunk!" Dave derided. "Might be someone just wants to leave us up in the air; wants us to start chasin' brick-tossers instead of lookin' for what really counts."

"That's a long shot guess," Gilroy thought. "And you're gambling with your life, boy. Next time it could be a bullet instead of a brick."

Dave stood up. "Excuse me, Lisa. Sheriff, sit down and have a cup of coffee with her while I take a look outside."

He went out to the sidewalk and stood by Slavin's coach. The passengers had embarked and Jake was now on the driver's seat. Mail and express were loaded.

"Giddap!" Jake cracked his whip and the horses moved off, heading east out of Main Street to take the Lemhi Pass trail.

Dave kept his eyes on the street. Saloons weren't open yet. The two big general stores, Shoup's and Andrews', were getting ready for the day's trade. A boy was sweeping off Shoup's walk. The town barber came along and unlocked his shop.

The two rooming houses were on side streets where Dave couldn't see them. Hitchracks were empty at this hour. Yet he had a feeling of being watched. Whether the brickbat note was a threat or only a bluff, the thrower could be watching to see the result.

He could be watching from some vantage point along the street; or even from a window of this hotel. In either case he'd know by now that Dave hadn't left on the stage.

Dave's eyes kept sweeping the street, from right to left. In a moment he became aware of another pair of eyes looking back at him. A lean, gunslung man stood just inside the entrance of Kingsbury's stable. The shadow of the entrance darkened him, so that Dave saw only that he wore a peaked black hat and the leathers of a rangeman.

Being rigged for the saddle he was probably a customer who'd just stabled his horse or was on the point of leaving. Nor did his fixed stare on Dave prove anything. Many curious eyes had fixed on Dave since noon yesterday, when he'd raced up to stop a jailyard hanging.

Yet something vaguely familiar about the man kept Dave from turning away. Perhaps he'd seen the man at some bar while making the rounds with Gilroy.

Suddenly Dave placed him. He remembered the company in Sunderlin's stage station at the midday-meal stop on Agency Creek. The people of two passing stages, the hotel, bar and corral crew, and a few stray guests like Smiley. Among them had been a strayman, two prospectors and a wolfer.

The man standing just inside Kingsbury's barn looked like the wolfer. The fact that he was there might be just a happenso — or it might tie a thread.

Dave stepped off the walk and angled across the street toward him. He half expected the man to retreat from sight. But he stood his ground till Dave came face to face with him. "Remember me?" Dave questioned.

The man was paper thin and his bony face had a three-day beard. His eyes fixed on Dave's badge, then dropped to Dave's holstered gun. "Can't say's I do." His voice was toneless. "Just got in a few minutes ago."

"Where did you leave your traps? They tell me you're a wolfer."

"Not with traps," the man said. "It's cheaper to use strychnine."

"Mind tellin' me your name?"

The wolfer shrugged. "Why not? I'm Frank Budlong. If it's any of my business, who're *you*?"

"I'm Harbison, a new deputy. Saw you at Sunderlin's day before yesterday. Quite a crowd there, remember? Have they got any ideas about who held up the stage?"

The man smiled cautiously. "It still had 'em buffaloed, when I left there. Got any ideas yourself?"

"I'm beginning to get one," Dave said.

"Such as what?" The wolfer's voice grew cagey.

"I figure it took *two* men to hold up that stage. One to put up openly at Sunderlin's roadhouse while the other camped out of sight across the creek."

"Yeh? Why would they do that?"

"The man inside could hear talk about a reprieve. Then he could slip across the creek and tip the camper. The camper could ride a mile downcreek and bushwhack the stage when it came along."

The man calling himself Budlong stood silently for a moment, with the narrow-eyed alertness of a man wrestling with a decision. Dave sensed it and wondered what chance he'd have if the man drew. He remembered a stray remark he'd heard from an oldtimer at Hailey. According to the old-timer, a favorite trick of a horse thief was to claim to be a wolfer; it made a convenient way to explain why he had no ranching or mining connection; and why he was riding some dim lonely trail.

"That's a right smart way to figger it," the man said finally. "There was talk of camp smoke across the creek, but nobody saw a camper. Guess I'd better go saddle up now."

It seemed to be a slip and Dave jumped on it. His sharp question stopped Budlong as the man was turning toward the stalls. "You said you just hit town a few minutes ago; so why saddle up again?"

When the wolfer spun about he looked dangerous. "I come and go as I please, mister. You figger to stop me?"

"Not if you'll let me look at your hands," Dave offered. "Just hold 'em out, palms up. If I'm wrong, I'll apologize and buy your breakfast."

The man stared. "Whadda yuh mean, if you're wrong?"

"When a fella squeezes a brick," Dave suggested, "it's apt to leave a pink stain on the inside of his hand. He can scrub it off with soap and water, and maybe he did this time. Or maybe he didn't. Mind givin' me a look?"

Budlong's hands moved, but not palms up. He went for his gun and Dave, half expecting it, crowded him chest to chest. As he closed in Dave raised an uppercut punch to the chin. It lifted Budlong from his heels and made the half-drawn gun go off. A wild bullet chipped the sill of the barn door.

Before he could shoot again Dave rocked him with a hook that sent him reeling. He followed with a head-on dive to the stomach. The barn's attendant came running from a grain room at the back; and racing from the hotel came Sheriff Gilroy.

They found Dave sitting astride a man in the barn's runway. Dave had two guns, his own and Budlong's. "I'm betting he tossed the brick, Sheriff."

But when they looked at the wolfer's hands they were clean.

CHAPTER
EIGHT

Dave turned Budlong over to Gilroy and went back to the hotel. The people there had heard the shot. He found Lisa in the lobby with Laura Kane. "What happened? Who was it?" Lisa asked anxiously.

"A wolfer named Budlong. Might be a break. Can't prove anything yet. I better get those newspapers for you, Lisa. Where do you want 'em?"

After consulting with Mrs. Kane it was decided that the reading could be done in Lisa's room. Dave went up to his own and got the pasteboard-bound file. The two women were waiting in Lisa's room, which faced both Main and Andrews Street. "Did you say a break?" the older woman asked keenly.

"Might be. There's a chance he was in on the deal to delay the telegram. But don't count on it. I'm off to help Gilroy shake him down."

He hurried to the sheriff's office where Gilroy was pumping questions. The man gave sullen, clipped answers.

"You drew a gun on a county officer, Budlong. Why?"

"He was pushin' me around."

"Why did you lie to him?"

"I didn't."

"You said you just hit town a few minutes ago."

"No such thing. I said I just got *in* a few minutes ago."

Dave admitted it with a grimace. "I thought he meant he'd just got in town; but he could've meant he'd just got in the stable."

"When *did* you hit town, Budlong?"

"A little before midnight. Took a bed at Cooper's roomin' house. Slept double with Jack Ferris."

"We'll ask Jack about it," Gilroy said. "What do you do when you're not wolfing?"

"Ranch jobs, mostly. Last one I had was at the Kaybar."

Gilroy turned to Dave. "That's Marvin Kane's outfit. Better check with Kane. Turn left at St. Charles Street; it's a small white cottage in the second block. Ask Marv if this guy ever worked for him. On your way back stop at Cooper's rooming house."

Dave went out and had no trouble finding the Kane town cottage. Its front yard had lilacs and its windows had ruffled yellow curtains. The look of homey neatness meant a woman's touch and Dave remembered Laura Kane.

His knock drew a prompt response. "Come in, Wes."

Dave opened the door and went in. "Just checking on a man named Budlong. Claims he used to work for you, Kane."

The stockman stood with a lathered face before a mirror. He was in pants and undershirt, with a steaming cup of coffee within reach. "Oh, it's you, Harbison!"

The tone was lazily cordial. "Wes Gordon went to saddle up and he's about due back. Budlong, you say?"

"He's on the carpet at Gilroy's office. What do you know about him?"

"Only that I took him on as a hand, coupla months ago. He wasn't any good. Fired him on the first payday. You think he gunned Ogle last night?"

"No. But maybe he heaved a brick through my window."

"Yeh?" The cattleman, still shaving at the mirror, cocked an eye. "Wes didn't say anything about a brick. I was asleep when he came in last night. When we got up he told me about Ogle."

"He was killed with a forty-four." Kane's gun hung holstered from a hook, and Dave saw that it was a forty-five.

"Yeh, that's what Wes said. Pour yourself some coffee, Harbison."

Dave helped himself and sat down. As he drank the coffee he looked narrowly at Kane. The man seemed vigorous and healthy; neither his skin nor his eyes showed any sign of dissipation. According to local talk he'd quit drinking more than a year ago.

Kane wiped his razor on a towel. "Anything I can do, Harbison, just let me know."

"You can begin," Dave said, "by telling me what you remember about my brother Gregg."

Kane finished at the mirror and put on a shirt. Then he rolled a cigarette, his eyes reminiscing. "He was a top hand and we all liked him. We hoped he'd stay on through the winter."

76

"Why didn't he?"

The rancher shrugged. "Who knows? Why does any cowboy ride on over the hill? This one packed his kit and headed south right after the fall gather in '78. Took the Blackfoot road. I remember Laura and I stood at the gate, waving goodbye to him. He was a special favorite of Laura's and she's a prime judge of men. Later we learned that he got as far as our Meadow Creek line camp that night. It's a day by saddle south of the ranchhouse."

"How do you know he got that far?"

"Because in late fall we always keep a hand at that line camp, to turn back any Kaybar cattle that try to drift over the Gilmore rise. Laura reminded Gregg of it when we said goodbye. 'Why don't you stop all night with Chuck Spoffard?' she said. 'That way you can get a hot supper.'"

The name alerted Dave. "Spoffard? You mean that foofoorawed yellowhead who's running for sheriff?"

"That's right. He was just a Kaybar saddle hand in those days. That week he was on solo duty at the south line camp. Next time we saw Chuck we asked if Gregg had stopped overnight with him; he said yes. That's the last we ever saw of your brother; or heard of him till twenty months later, when we read about him getting shot down near Hailey."

"When did Spoffard quit you?"

"The spring of '80, I think. It was right after Laura . . ." Marvin Kane broke off and a grim dejection settled on his face.

"Right after your wife left you," Dave supplied quietly. "I know about that, Kane. Please don't think I'm poking into your personal life. I'm not interested in anything unless it touches Gregg, some way."

Kane gave him a quizzical look. "And you think Spoffard does?"

"Maybe. He was the last man who ever saw Gregg in this county. Twenty months later he quits a forty dollar job, buys a ranch and runs for sheriff. Where did he get the money?"

"On Gamblers' Row in Denver, he claims. Right after he quit us he went to Denver, stayed a month and came back flush. Said he'd had a big run of luck on Holladay Street there. He bought the Box Q and in the fall ran for sheriff against Gilroy."

"Gilroy beat him," Dave said. "But now it's two years later and he's trying again. How did he go to Denver?"

"The only way you could go, two years ago: by saddle to the end of the U.N. rails which was at Idaho Falls, then; and from there by train to Denver. Since then the U.N.'s built north into Montana."

Dave nodded. "I came on it myself as far as Red Rock. Thanks a lot, Kane."

He went out to the street just as Wesley Gordon rode up and tied two saddle mounts at the rack. Dave checked a date with him. "Look, Gordon; do you remember just when Chuck Spoffard quit the Kaybar?"

The cowboy squinted curiously. "Nope. I didn't keep books on him. All I remember is he went to Denver and hit a jackpot. When he got back there was a piece in the paper about it. You could look it up."

"Thanks." Another date nudged Dave's mind as he went back toward Main. The date of Gregg's murder in May two years ago. Spoffard, riding south toward Utah at about that time, could have gone by way of Hailey.

At Cooper's rooming house he made an inquiry and then moved on to the sheriff's office. "I locked that wolfer up," Gilroy told him, "till we decide what to do with him."

"Just like he said," Dave reported, "he got in at midnight and took a room at Cooper's. They doubled him up with Jack Ferris. Ferris woke up twice before morning; both times Budlong was in bed with him."

"What about the Kaybar job?"

"It only lasted a couple of weeks; then they fired him."

"I'll get fired myself," Gilroy growled, "if I don't start gettin' results. Spoffard'll snow me under, come election day."

"What about that guy Spoffard? Is he on the level?"

"He's a show-off," Gilroy said. "All the same folks figure he'd make a right good sheriff. He's smart, for one thing. And he's gun-fast; a heap handier with a gun than I am."

"Who did he ever gun?"

"Shot it out with a rustler one time, when he was riding for the Kaybar. He wins all the Fourth of July shooting matches. But look, boy; he couldn't've gunned Ogle last night. He was at Tony Sebastian's."

"Where did Ogle live?"

"He kept a shack about half a mile up the riverbank; a two-room shanty in a cottonwood grove."

"Maybe I'd better have a look at it," Dave suggested. "He told me he knew who killed my brother; said he had *proof!* Maybe the proof's stashed in that shanty."

"Go right ahead," Gilroy agreed. "Here's a ring of keys we took off Pinky. While you're at it, I'll go ask the county attorney what we'd better do with Budlong."

Dave went out and turned toward the river. Rearing gauntly in the jailyard was the scaffold built for Court Grady. Its shadow lay across the walk as Dave passed by. They'd leave it standing, naturally, since the reprieve was only for thirty days. Unless new evidence turned up it would still be needed.

It was a hideously foreboding thing which Lisa would see daily from her hotel window. For thirty wretched days the sight would torture her. The thought flogged Dave and made him feel guiltily impatient with his present errand. For running down Gregg's murder wouldn't help Lisa. There was no thirty-day deadline on solving it, like there was on the one which Grady was charged with. And anything he found at Ogle's shanty could hardly bear on the Grady case.

Passing a warehouse Dave saw a boy tacking a paper on its outer wall. And at the river bank he saw one just like it impaled on a cottonwood tree. It was a campaign poster announcing SPOFFARD FOR SHERIFF.

Others, no doubt, would be posted from end to end of the county. Chuck Spoffard would be hard to beat. Young, smart and gun-fast, he was a better mixer than Gilroy. While the tired, shabby old sheriff was riding dim trails and getting nowhere, Spoffard would be standing treat at a dozen bars.

Dave turned up the river bank and followed a path which soon took him past the last house. He came to the mouth of Lemhi Creek, crossed it on a foot bridge, and continued on up the wide, turbulent waters of the Salmon. Shortly the path brought him to a grove of cottonwoods shading an unpainted shanty. It was an untidy place, with rusty cans strewn about outside; its door was closed and the window shades drawn.

The first key Dave tried didn't fit the lock. Before trying another he turned the knob and found the door unlocked. Maybe Ogle had habitually left it unlocked because there was nothing inside worth stealing; or perhaps he'd intended to return here immediately after a quick call on Dave at the hotel.

Pushing the door open Dave entered a room with a straw matting on the floor and an unmade bed. There was a table with a lamp, a rocker, two stools and a table. A chest of drawers had a litter in front of it. An open doorway gave to a second room. Then Dave saw a trunk with another litter by it. Ogle, he thought, had been the world's worst housekeeper.

But as his eyes grew accustomed to the gloom Dave changed his mind. He saw that the chest drawers were empty. The bed was not only unmade; its mattress had been upturned and ripped open. A search had been going on here. A very recent search because a live cigarette butt lay on the floor.

Dave's hand moved to the grip of his gun and his eyes fixed on the inner doorway. He had a feeling that someone stood beyond it, waiting, ready to challenge him with a bullet. A man who'd been interrupted while ransacking this shanty.

For what? For proof which could fix the guilt of a two-year-old and far-away murder? More and more Dave felt sure that Pinky Ogle had first tried blackmail before coming to room number ten last night. The proof he'd mentioned would be hidden somewhere. In that case the other man would want to destroy it; he might come here himself for that purpose, or he could send an agent.

Dave waited a breathless minute for some sound beyond the inner doorway. He heard nothing. Yet here was a fresh cigarette and the litter of a search.

"Come on out!" Dave's command rang hollowly through the shanty. It brought no answer other than a stir of leaves in the grove and the splash of the racing river. If the other room had an outside door, perhaps the man had slipped out. "I got you covered!" Dave warned, and moved cautiously forward.

The faint creaking of a floor board told him the man was still in there. A man with a gun! He'd changed position for a more commanding control of the doorway. Yet Dave knew that if he went for help the man would get away. A man who was connected with the killing of Pinky Ogle, which meant he was probably also connected with the murder of Gregg Harbison!

A chance like this might never come again. Dave stiffened his nerve and moved on forward.

He reached the doorway with his heart pounding and his gun level. Through all his one year in Idaho he'd practiced with a gun, both for speed and accuracy, but this would be his first man-to-man gunfight.

Standing erect Dave called out sharply, "I'm coming in after you!"

Then he dropped quietly to his knees and one hand, hoping his voice had made the man look for him at full height rather than at floor level.

On knees and one hand Dave advanced till his eyes and his gun were through the doorway. Against a dim far wall he saw a tall, black-bearded gunman. By his build and his beard and his brown corduroy coat and his baggy pants Dave knew him. The surprise of it jarred his wits and made him lose a precious second. It was in that lost breath of time that the man's alert level eyes dropped to the doorway's threshold and saw Dave there.

The gun in his hand boomed twice; Dave's fired only once and wild. A brain-shattering hammer seemed to crash on Dave's head. He flattened in the doorway, stunned and bleeding. Outside the rapids of the river rushed by and leaves overhead rustled in the wind. But Dave heard nothing, knew nothing of the passage of time.

CHAPTER
NINE

He came to consciousness in his room at the hotel. Slowly and groggily he came out of his stupor to find his head bandaged and four people in the room. Two were men and two were women. "I think he's coming out of it, Doctor." The voice was Laura Kane's.

A man leaning over the bed had pince-nez glasses and a pointed beard. "You're going to be all right," he said. "Just stay quiet a few days. I'll look in again tomorrow."

By the time he was gone Dave knew that the others were Lisa Grady and the sheriff. Gilroy said: "The slug dug a ditch down your scalp, boy. Only skin deep, the doc says, but you lost a lot of blood."

"What happened?" Dave asked weakly.

"That's for *you* to say. When you didn't come back I went lookin' for you. Found you gunned in Pinky's shack."

"Doctor Flint," Lisa interposed, "says we mustn't excite him."

"One question won't hurt," Gilroy said. "Who gunned you, Dave?"

Dave hadn't gathered his wits enough to answer. As his head slowly cleared, the sheriff paced impatiently.

"Who was it, boy? The same guy who gunned Ogle, I'll bet."

Dave gave a pale smile and shook his head.

"Then who the devil was it?" the sheriff demanded.

"Brushy-Chin," Dave said.

Gilroy stared. "You mean the guy who held up that stage?"

As Dave nodded, the sheriff's mouth hung open in complete stupefaction. The same outright astonishment showed on Lisa Grady's face. And on Laura Kane's. "But why should *he* be there?" Laura exclaimed.

"Are you sure it was *him?*" Gilroy prodded.

Again Dave nodded. "Brushy chin, brown corduroy coat, baggy pants. The same man who held up Jake's stage."

"But what was *he* doin' in Pinky's shack?" Gilroy wondered. "Turnin' it upside down like that?"

Yet when he concentrated on it the significance of it couldn't be missed. Dave looked at Lisa and saw it dawn in her eyes; then in Laura Kane's; last of all in Ad Gilroy's.

"Well I'll golly-be-darned!" the sheriff muttered under his breath. "The same guy, huh! The one who slapped you in Smiley's dugout!"

"Nobody else." Dave's head was almost clear now.

"Was he masked this time?" Lisa asked.

Dave shook his head. The effort made it ache a little and his hand went to a bandage there. "He wasn't expecting anyone to come in. When I did, he had to shoot his way out."

It wasn't necessary to draw a diagram. In a little while Gilroy put it into words. "He delayed that reprieve to keep it from saving your dad, Lisa. And he frisked Pinky's shack to destroy proof about who killed your brother, Dave. Means there's a link between those two cases. If we break either one of them, we're likely to clean up the other."

"Maybe not as simple as that," Dave said. "But there's a tie-up, all right. Strings reaching two ways — one back to a shooting down south two years ago, the other to a killing two months ago in this county. And the same man or gang of men is pulling both strings."

Putting it that way made him feel closer to Lisa. Her cause was his own now.

Dave rested quietly till noon. Then Chung the little Chinese bartender came in with a bowl of broth. He sat on the edge of the bed and fed Dave with a spoon.

Six hours later he came again, this time bringing supper on a tray. He put pillows behind Dave and propped him up. "Mr. Booth comes to see you but the ladies will not let him disturb."

"Where are they, Chung?"

"They read with the door open."

"You mean they're reading those old newspapers?"

The little bartender nodded. "When people come to disturb you they will not permit."

"Tell 'em I'm okay, Chung, and lonesome for company."

He was hoping Lisa would come. But it was Laura Kane who, an hour after nightfall, came in with a glass of port wine. "The doctor thinks it may make you sleep."

She started to leave him but Dave begged her to sit down. "Tell me about my brother Gregg, please. Anything you can remember about those six months he was at the ranch."

She was slow to answer. When she did she seemed to choose the words carefully. "He was a good worker, strong and capable. A kind man and a gay man and lots of fun to have around." She hesitated a moment, then added, "He was almost like one of the family."

Dave watched her shrewdly. Why had she put it that way? "Yet after he left you never heard from him again? Not even a post card?"

"No. Cowboys, I suppose, hardly ever write letters. Unless it's a business letter. And your brother left no unfinished business up here."

"I've talked with your husband. I mean your ex-husband. He said you both waved goodbye to Gregg; he said Gregg got as far as your south line camp that day; he spent the night with Chuck Spoffard there. So Spoffard was the last Lemhi County person to see him."

To his complete surprise she corrected him. "No, Dave. Because a few minutes ago Lisa and I found this in an old newspaper. We've been reading all day, you know." She brought a notation from her purse. "Lisa said not to bother you with it till tomorrow. But I think you'd better see it now."

The item had been copied from the October 20, 1878, issue of the Salmon City newspaper. Dave read it silently.

Pinky Ogle drove in last night from Blackfoot with a load of liquor for his river-front bar. He says the trip took him six days each way. Coming back he stopped overnight at the Kaybar and says the Kaybar cattle are rolling in fat. We hope you have a good winter, Kaybar.

When Dave looked askance at Laura she explained. "It was four years ago and I'd naturally forget about Ogle stopping overnight with us. But this item makes me remember it. It was two nights after your brother left us. And I remember Ogle mentioned that he passed Gregg on the road, at the top of Birch Creek, a few miles beyond our south line camp."

"Is that all?"

"That's all. But it means Ogle, not Spoffard, was the last local man to see Gregg. And now Ogle . . ."

"And now Ogle," Dave took up shrewdly, "gets shot for claiming to know who killed my brother."

"But it was all so long ago!" Laura Kane murmured.

"Forty-six months in all," Dave calculated. "Twenty from then till Gregg's murder at Hailey; and another twenty-six till now. What else did you and Lisa find in those old papers?"

"Let's save it for tomorrow." Laura smiled a goodnight and left him.

The wine did help bring sleep. Dave wakened in the morning to find Chung there with towels and hot water. Deftly he washed and shaved Dave. "One time in San Francisco," he grinned, "I am a valet."

A waitress brought a breakfast tray and Chung remained to feed Dave. "Anything happen last night, Chung? Any more shooting?"

"The only shooting," Chung said, "is with the mouth. My bar is full last night and there is much talk. Many times Mr. Chuck buys drinks for all customers. He hopes they will make him sheriff."

"Bet I know what his line is. He tells 'em Gilroy's a bumbling old flubdudder missing every trick; but if they'll just elect Mr. Chuck, things'll be different."

"Many believe him!" Chung said.

Later the doctor appeared to re-dress the head wound. "Keep quiet one more day and night," he ordered. "Then I'll let you stir around a little."

After he left, Booth of the *Recorder* came in. He was full of questions but Dave got in the first one. "Has that deputy come back from Sunderlin's?"

"Not yet. Why?"

"I want to know if he dopes it out like I do: that it took two men to hold up the stage. One mixing with the station people, like the wolfer did, and the other camping out of sight across the creek."

The editor rubbed his chin. "Makes sense," he admitted. "It's the only way the holdup man could find out the reprieve was on the stage. The catch is — why were they waiting for it?"

The point had puzzled Dave and he could only guess. "If someone had a good reason to want the hanging to come off on schedule, he might go a long way to make sure of it. Like sending a couple of guys to bushwhack some last minute telegram from the governor. He'd know Lisa Grady's been begging for one ever since the trial."

"He'd know too," Booth added, "that a year ago Governor Neil actually did send a last minute reprieve in the Sam Kidgeines case. And that someone held up the Boise-to-Hailey stage to delay it."

"If we're right," Dave brooded, "I nominate Budlong for the inside man. The outside man was the guy who gunned me in Ogle's shanty. Is Budlong still locked up?"

The editor nodded. "But the only charge they can book him on is resisting a county deputy. At the worst he's only an errand boy for someone else."

"Like Tony Sebastian?"

"Maybe. Tony had a five-thousand-dollar motive and he could have hired those fellows for five hundred."

"Have Kane and his man Gordon gone back to the Kaybar?"

"Not yet. They were about to leave when a cattle buyer named Whipple braced them about contracting the Kaybar calf crop this fall. So they'll stay in town another day to dicker on it."

Through the Main Street window Dave could see the top half of a gallows tower in the jailyard. It pulled his mind back to Lisa. Two days of the thirty-day reprieve had slipped relentlessly by. "Look, Mr. Booth. Tell me about that alibi witness of Grady's."

The editor shrugged. "He claims he was milking his cow, right after sunup that morning, when a stranger stopped by and asked him the way to Haystack Mountain. Grady claims he fished a scrap of paper from his pocket and drew a sketch. By following it the man could ride down the Lemhi to Salmon City, then ride the Yellowjacket stage road over the hump to Leesburg, then head up Camp Creek a few miles to Haystack Mountain. The stranger thanked him and rode away."

"Did Grady describe him?"

"Yep. Said he was a skinny little man about sixty years old with a gold front tooth. His horse was a piebald buckskin and his saddle was an old army McClellan."

"And no one believed him?"

"How could they? The sheriff raked that route over from end to end and nobody saw a stranger like that. He'd have had to pass through both Salmon City and Leesburg. He didn't. Nobody up around Haystack Mountain ever heard of a man like that."

"Do me a favor, Mr. Booth. Lisa's reading the 1878 file for me. When she gets through, take it back and give her the one for '79. Then the files for '80, '81 and right on up to date."

"Will do," the *Recorder* man promised.

Later in the day Lisa came in with a notebook. She looked fresh and cool in a starched white dress and she sat down like a brisk, impersonal secretary. "In addition to the one you found yourself," she reported, "we came across eight items which mention your brother, people at the Kaybar, or Pinky Ogle. Shall I read them aloud?"

"Please," Dave said.

"Item 2 tells about a roping contest in town here." Lisa read from her book:

. . . The finalists were Wes Gordon and Gregg Harbison of the Kaybar. It was close, but Harbison won out and picked up the cash prize of $25.00. Better luck next year, Wes.

"Roping was a pet hobby of Gregg's," Dave recalled, "even back on the Missouri farm."

Without interruption Lisa read five more items.

#3 Aug 4 1878
A gala dance Saturday night at the Junction school house. Music by the Salmon City string band. Laura and Marv Kane led the grand march. Chuck Spoffard distinguished himself when one of the fair sex fainted in the ladies' cloak room where she'd come upon a coiled rattlesnake. Chuck rushed in and shot the reptile's head off. Nice shooting, Chuck.

#4 Aug 18 1878
Job Whipple, cattle buyer, has been at the Kaybar looking for young beef. Gregg Harbison showed him around the range.

#5 Sept 1 1878
Laura Kane came in for the weekend. She will sing a solo at the Methodist Church Sunday. Gregg Harbison drove her in. Mighty sweet of you, Laura, to ride a seventy-mile round trip just to sing one anthem for us.

#6 Sept 15 1878
Trouble at the Kaybar! Whatever it was Pres Werner said to Gregg Harbison on the bunkhouse steps, he probably regrets it now. It seems Gregg sent a fast one to the chin and they had to carry Pres to his bunk. We hope you've cooled off by this time, boys.

#7 Oct 10 1878
Word comes from the Kaybar that the fall gather is over. Marvin says his tally book shows a nice increase. Only thing wrong, he says, is that he's losing a top hand. Gregg Harbison is packing his kit to ride on. Come back and see us some time, Gregg.

#8 Oct 20 1878
Pinky Ogle got back from Blackfoot with a . . .

"Mrs. Kane," Dave broke in, "showed me that one last night. Ogle, driving north, passed Gregg riding south on the Blackfoot road. But let's go back to Number 6. What did Werner say that made Gregg poke him one? Did you ask Mrs. Kane?"

Lisa nodded. "She says she wasn't at home at the time. But she's sure it wasn't anything important because when your brother left, a month later, he was on good terms with everybody, including Werner."

"Something funny about it!" Dave brooded. "Gregg wasn't the kind to fly off the handle and throw punches."

"Why don't you ask one of the crew?"

"They tell me Wes Gordon's the only hand left there from Gregg's time. I'll ask him. I can ask Chuck Spoffard too; and Kane himself. Look, Lisa. I'm stuck in bed here. If you see any of those three will you ask him to come in a minute?"

The girl promised she would. "I'll leave this with you Dave." She handed him the notebook. "Now I must take that file back to Mr. Booth and get the one for 1879."

Dave didn't see her again all day. Laura Kane came in once, with a glass of port, and Chung twice with trays of food.

Soon after supper Wesley Gordon came in and stood by the bed, short, stocky and gunslung. "Miss Grady says you wanta see me."

Dave read item 6 aloud to him, then asked, "What the dickens did Werner say to my brother, to make him get mad like that?"

Gordon shrugged. "How would I know? It was four years ago. Lots of plain and fancy joshing goes on around a bunk-shack. Sometimes it gets under a guy's skin and he goes on the prod for a minute."

"You're sure Werner never held a grudge against Gregg?"

"Dead sure of it. You're barkin' up a wrong tree, fella."

"Is Werner still in the county?"

"Don't think so. Last I heard he was in Wyoming. I'd forget it, if I was you, Harbison."

When he left, Dave had a feeling he'd been brushed off. Why did Gordon want him to forget that flare-up with Pres Werner? Would it be the same if he asked Marvin Kane? Maybe he'd stumbled on a skeleton which the Kaybar wanted to keep locked up!

It was some hours later when Sheriff Gilroy came in. He looked haggard and discouraged. "Been at it all day, Dave. Got a hatful of suspicions but can't prove nary a one."

Dave showed him item 6. "Do you know where Pres Werner is now?"

"Sure. He's tendin' bar down at Shoup. Couple of months ago he came up for jury duty. Served as juryman at the Grady trial."

Dave's eyes narrowed. "I suppose most everyone in the county looked in at that trial. Including the Kaybar boys."

"Sure they did. Why?"

So Wes Gordon would have seen his old bunkmate, Werner, on the jury! In any case he'd be sure to know that Werner had a job tending bar at a mining camp only forty miles down the river. It meant Gordon had ducked the question. He didn't want Dave to dig up the reason for a punch thrown four years ago at the Kaybar.

"Is your other deputy back yet, Sheriff?"

"I look for him back tomorrow," Gilroy said. "Name's Blanchard. Worst of it is my jailer's laid up with lumbago. Till either him or you or Blanchard joins me, I gotta do everything myself."

The sheriff went out and closed the door. As he turned down the hall he heard voices. Lisa's and Laura Kane's. They were reading old newspapers and making notes. Not stopping, Gilroy went down to the street and on to his jail office.

There he stepped through a doorway into a cell corridor for a goodnight look at his two prisoners, Court Grady and Frank Budlong.

Something round and cold and steel-hard punched into his back. A voice behind him said, "Keep your mouth shut, old man."

"What do you want?" The dullness of Gilroy's tone measured his sense of defeat and humiliation. To be held up in his own jail! Chuck Spoffard, campaigning these next two months, would ridicule him at every bar and cracker barrel in the county.

"Take out your keys." The gun punched harder. "Then let Budlong out."

Gilroy had no choice. He unlocked Budlong's cell. He knew they'd leave by a back door and not be seen on the street.

But the sheriff himself got one quick look. He twisted enough to see that the man with the gun had a brushy chin, and wore a brown corduroy coat over baggy pants. This was the Agency Creek holdup man who'd later shot his way past Dave at Ogle's shanty.

"Go to sleep, Sheriff!" The gun crashed on Gilroy's head and bashed him senseless to the floor.

CHAPTER
TEN

Dave dozed a little while and was awakened by a disturbance down the hall. Someone stumbled and a man said, "Easy does it. Joe."

"It's the second door on the right," another said. "Here comes Doc Flint." A door down the hall opened, then closed.

A saloon fight, Dave supposed. One of the hotel guests had come out second best and they'd carried him up to his room.

When next Dave wakened the morning sun was on his window. Chung appeared with hot water and towels. Later he brought oatmeal and scrambled eggs.

Dave's next caller was a mountain of flesh wearing a brass badge. The man looked sixty pounds too heavy for the saddle, yet he wore spurs and riding boots. He had sleepy blue eyes and plump ruddy cheeks from which three chins receded downward into a number nineteen collar. Being bigger at the middle than anywhere else, his pants were supported by suspenders.

"More grief!" he said. "If it ain't one thing it's another."

"You're Blanchard?"

"That's me. Buck Blanchard. You heard about Gilroy?"

"What about him?"

"I got in from Sunderlin's at midnight and found him on the jail floor. Somebody batted him on the bean and turned loose that wolfer. Doc Flint's with him now."

Dave swung his legs out of bed and reached for his socks. But Blanchard, with a giant's strength, pushed him back. "Not today, pardner. The doc just gave me orders."

"But they'll get away!" Dave protested. "Budlong and that . . ."

"They've already got away." Blanchard pinioned Dave to the bed and went on in a mild drawl: "Tomorrow's another day. You got a ditch down your noggin and Gilroy's got a goose-egg bump. Me, I'm dead on my feet and won't be worth shootin' till I get some sleep. So today we take it easy; tomorrow we go to work."

"Did you find out anything at Sunderlin's?"

"Nothin' 'cept what you've already doped out: that it was Brushy-Chin and that wolfer. It was Brushy-Chin who conked the boss last night. I ordered breakfast sent up here, pardner. We can talk while I eat."

The breakfast proved to be steak, six eggs and a stack of pancakes. The massive deputy dug in heartily. "Begin at the start, pardner."

Dave outlined everything he knew or suspected, explained the apparent link between Grady's case and his brother's, then showed the eight items copied from 1878 newspapers.

"It smells like Tony Sebastian," Blanchard mumbled through a mouthful of food. "Whatta yuh say I go bulldog him?"

"If he's back of it he won't admit it," Dave objected. "You'd do better with that redhead hostess of his, Cherry. She had a loose tongue, last I saw of her. Butter her up with a few drinks and maybe she'll get chummy."

"I'll give her a play. What else, pardner?"

"Find out who else was on the Kaybar crew four years ago. If you run into any of them, ask 'em why my brother had that row with Werner."

"I'll hop to it soon as I get a little shut-eye." Buck Blanchard finished his breakfast and went out.

Presently the doctor came in and took off Dave's bandage. Under it was a strip of tape which had been pasted along a scalp furrow. His reflection in a mirror made Dave grimace. "Golly! I look like a half-bald owl!"

"It won't show with your hat on," Flint said. "Stay in bed till five o'clock, boy. After that you're on your own."

"How's Gilroy?"

"I told him the same thing. Both of you'll live till the next bullet comes along."

Before noon Dave had one more caller. Booth of the *Weekly Recorder*. "Anything I can do, young fella?"

"Sure. Help Blanchard find out who worked for the Kaybar in '78."

"That's easy. It was an election year and I copied down every ranch payroll in the county, so I could brace 'em to vote for my slate. The cook out there was Packy Blue, I remember. He quit not long ago and opened up an eating house at Leesburg."

Dave made a note of it. "Happen to remember anyone else?"

"Offhand I can't think of anyone but Blue and Gordon and Werner. And Chuck Spoffard of course. I'll look it up and check with you again."

Lisa didn't appear all day. Dave watched the clock, minute by minute, and at five he bounced out of bed. Shortly he was dressed. All but his gunbelt and gun. He suspected they'd taken them to keep him in his room.

He looked out at Main Street and saw dust rising under the hooves of a bull train pulling in from the railhead. Otherwise the town seemed relatively quiet. Knots of men stood in subdued talk. Beyond them reared a gallows tower, grim in the jailyard, relentless reminder of a deadline creeping nearer every hour. Three days of the reprieve were gone now. For the Gradys, the rest of them would be like sand trickling through an hour glass.

Lisa, from her own window, day after day would look out at that same ugly reminder. Abruptly Dave left his room, crossed the hall and knocked at her door.

"Come in," she said.

He found her with an open news file in front of her. She didn't seem surprised at seeing him. "I knew you'd be up, Dave. You're restless, just like I am."

He grinned when he saw her looking at his mutilated hair. "Maybe we'd better go outdoors so I can put on my hat."

Lisa looked down at the 1879 news file. "I've been reading all day," she said. "So far there's not a single mention of your brother; or of Pinky Ogle."

"What about the Kaybar folks?"

"Only one item. It's a sort of preachy editorial. Listen." Lisa read it from her notebook.

#9 Apr 6 1879
It always makes us sad when a man we like starts riding a dark brown whisky sulk instead of his saddle. We wish he'd snap out of it. We wish we had a ranch half as good as his, and a wife half as pretty as his; and if we did we sure wouldn't spend our time hanging around the Salmon City bars. We wish we knew what the trouble was; but one thing we *do* know; the cure for it doesn't come in a bottle.

"It's about Marvin Kane?" Dave asked.

"Judge for yourself," Lisa said. "Laura was with me when I found it. She made an excuse to leave and I haven't seen her since."

Dave looked at the date, April 1879. "According to Booth she stuck with him a year longer. Until the spring of '80."

101

"He doesn't look like a heavy drinker," Lisa said.

"Booth says he quit right after Laura left him. Now he's trying to get her back. Is he having any luck?"

"I'm sure he isn't. When his name comes up she either walks out or changes the subject. Tonight she has a supper date with her broker, Mr. Garside."

"What about you having one with me?"

Her brief smile chased the shadow of tragedy from her face. "I'll be ready at six," she said.

Shortly after six they went into the dining room together. A waitress placed them at a table for two; so Deputy Blanchard, when he came along a little later, had to make his report standing. "I asked two people about that fracas at the Kaybar; Marv Kane and Wes Gordon. Marv claims he can't remember it; Wes says Werner ribbed your brother about gettin' bucked off a horse; made your brother sore for a minute, Wes says."

"What about that redhead at Sebastian's?"

"Can't get a thing out of her, so far. I'll try again."

"Who's watching the jail?"

"Pop Sweeney's back on duty. His lumbago's a mite better."

As Blanchard moved on Dave turned to Lisa. "It just don't wash down. Gregg wouldn't get fighting mad because someone ribbed him for getting bucked off a horse."

Another guest came in. As he passed by Lisa spoke to him. "Good evening, Mr. Mitchell."

102

It was the local assayer who'd been penned overnight in a dugout with Dave. After a nod to Lisa he said, "How are you doing, Harbison?"

Dave looked up with a grin. "As good as new. What happened to that bear hunt of yours?"

"Chuck put it off a month," Mitchell explained. "Said he's too busy campaigning right now."

"Chuck Spoffard?"

"That's right. It was Chuck who organized it. He's furnishing the pack stock, so it's up to him to say when and where we go. I guess those Geerston Creek grizzlies'll keep a month longer."

Mitchell moved on leaving Dave with a furrow of puzzlement. "It's a long time till election day. Spoffard'll be just as busy campaigning next month as he is now."

"Mr. Garside was telling Laura about that hunt," Lisa remembered. "He was all ready to go when Mr. Spoffard postponed it."

"How many were going?"

"Four or five, I think he said. A lawyer named Lillard. Mr. Booth was invited, too. Is it important?"

Dave shrugged. "I suppose not. It's just that Spoffard's name keeps popping up all the time, in funny places."

Marvin Kane appeared and looked around the dining room as though he expected to meet someone. Dave heard him speak to a waitress. "Has Wes Gordon shown up, Molly? I told him to meet me here."

"I haven't seen him, Mr. Kane."

The Kaybar owner seemed mildly annoyed as he sat down to eat alone. Then Laura Kane came in with Matt Garside. As they passed Kane's table the rancher spoke eagerly to Laura. Her response was an unsmiling nod.

"I wouldn't give much for his chances," Dave said.

The supper hour passed and Wes Gordon didn't join his employer. The fact seemed to puzzle Kane. Passing out through the lobby Dave heard him say to the clerk, "If you see Gordon, send him over to the cottage."

Dave and Lisa went out on the Main Street porch to watch the stages come in. The coach from Red Rock was on time but the stage from the west was late. "It usually is," Lisa said.

Dave gazed thoughtfully after the tall, stalwart figure of Marvin Kane as it receded up the walk. What unforgivable thing had the man done? On the surface it seemed clear enough. Husband becomes a drunkard; wife divorces him; the man reforms; but the woman won't take him back.

Was it that simple? Or was there a deeper, more sinister barrier between them?

Dark came to the street and a shabby conveyance from Leesburg rattled in. They called it the Yellowjacket stage but actually it was only a canvas-covered spring wagon. Dave saw it stop at the express office in the next block. "Is it a daily?" he asked.

Lisa shook her head. "It goes out one day and comes back the next. Runs through Leesburg and on to a camp on Yellowjacket Creek. Mr. Garside says it's the roughest trail in Idaho."

"It sure is, Miss." The bulk of Buck Blanchard appeared on the porch by them. "The roughest and the steepest and the crookedest. And pretty soon it'll be the loneliest. The cream's been skimmed off that basin. They've brought out sixteen million in placer gold since Eli Mulkey panned the first color on Nappias Creek, back in '66. Leesburg boomed big for a few years but she's thinnin' out now."

A hazy thought was teasing Dave. "Look, Buck. Wes Gordon was supposed to meet his boss for supper but he didn't show up. I wonder if he left town."

"Why would he leave town?"

"Maybe so he wouldn't have to answer any more embarrassing questions. I mean about a ruckus between Werner and my brother four years ago. Might be more important than we think."

"Easy enough to find out," Blanchard said. "We can look in Kingsbury's stable and see'f his horse is still there."

"Let's do it," Dave said. "Excuse me a minute, Lisa."

He went over to the livery barn with Blanchard. Hanging lamps lighted the runway where the night man was forking straw bedding into stalls. "Is Wes Gordon's horse here?" Blanchard inquired.

"Not since five o'clock. He came in for it about then and rode off."

"By himself?"

The attendant nodded. "I ast if he wanted Marvin Kane's horse too, but he said no." He thumbed toward a rangy sorrel in a nearby stall.

The sorrel had four white stockings and was branded *LD* on the left hip. The brand caught Dave's eye and he vaguely remembered having seen it before.

Buck Blanchard cocked an eye. "Left about five, huh! I was with him myself about ten minutes before that." His eyes narrowed as they met Dave's.

The timing could mean something. At four-fifty Gordon was asked a disturbing question. At five he left town, breaking a supper date with his boss. Was he covering up?

Dave was still looking at the *LD* on the sorrel's hip. "Is it a local brand?" he asked.

"Nope," the liveryman said. "A south Idaho outfit, I think. Marv Kane's been ridin' that sorrel for a couple of years now. Likely some horse trader came through and swapped it to him."

All at once Dave remembered. There was an *LD* ranch not far from Hailey where he'd spent many futile months making inquiries about Gregg's murder. And again the timing could mean something. At about the time of Gregg's murder a horse from that locality had come into Marvin Kane's possession!

Dave went into the stall for a closer look. He even examined the sorrel's teeth for age. Then he led Blanchard to the street. "Let's go write a letter, Buck. A bee's abuzzin' under my hat."

He crossed to the hotel and spoke briefly to Lisa. Then he rejoined Blanchard and they hurried to the sheriff's office.

Buck pointed to a writing desk. "Plenty of letter heads in the top drawer. Help yourself, pardner."

Dave addressed an envelope to the manager of the *LD* ranch, Hailey, Idaho Territory. The note he enclosed said:

Dear Sir:

A seven-year-old sorrel gelding bearing your brand is on this range. Animal has four white stockings. Has been in Lemhi County about two years. Please inform us when and to whom you sold same.

Truly yours,
Ad Gilroy, Sheriff
Salmon City, I.T.

Dave sealed the envelope. "Where's the post office, Buck?"

It was in the next block toward the river and Buck led him there. "If you poke it through the slot now it'll go out on the morning stage."

As they posted the letter, something he saw on the river bank alerted Buck Blanchard. "Look, pardner!" He pointed, then walked rapidly that way.

Dave kept pace with him. Just below the river bridge at the foot of Main, a low flat-roofed building made a dark silhouette against the night. It was Pinky Ogle's bar and poker parlor — a place which had been closed and locked since his death. "But looks like someone busted in, pardner." Buck lengthened his stride.

This time Dave saw it. The flicker of a candle beyond a window. A moving candle. Someone was prowling the place. And why not? Brushy-Chin had prowled Pinky's shanty for something he'd failed to find there — a thing which just as easily could be hidden at the dead man's place of business.

The building had two doors, one facing the town and the other facing the river. "You watch this side, pardner; I'll take the other." Blanchard went charging around to the wharf side and Dave took his stand. The door at hand hadn't been crashed. Window panes were now dark. Maybe the prowler had heard an approach and snuffed his candle.

A minute passed. The broad Salmon River hummed by and in the dim night light Dave saw a tarp-covered scow moored at the wharf. Then he heard what sounded like Blanchard making an entry from the other side. He heard Buck's shout: "Come on outa there, fella!"

The door on Dave's side burst open and a man darted forth. He was a small man with a dark, sharp face, a full head shorter than Brushy-Chin. He cannon-balled out and his head struck Dave's middle. Dave doubled and went flat. He made a wild snatch for an ankle as the man charged over him, heading north along the river bank.

A gun roared three times and for a dizzy moment Dave wasn't sure who was shooting. Blood on his finger was from a cut made by a spur on the ankle he'd snatched at. When he got to his feet Blanchard stood by him blazing away at a dim, scurrying shape which a breath later faded into the river willows.

CHAPTER
ELEVEN

Buck Blanchard gave chase, all three hundred pounds of him. He was too heavy for speed and soon gave up, angry and winded.

"Makes four of 'em," Dave muttered. He meant that tonight's prowler had too small a build to be either Budlong, Brushy-Chin or the man who'd shot Ogle through an open window.

"Makes five," Buck argued, "if you wanta count the guy who tossed a brick in on you."

"It proves they didn't find anything at the shanty, Buck. So whatever they're looking for is still stashed somewhere."

"You go tell Gilroy, pardner, while I work the joint over."

Dave hurried to the hotel and to Gilroy's room. The sheriff was sitting up in bed with a bump on his head. "How you doin', Sheriff?"

"All spavined and runnin' last," Gilroy growled. "It's beginning to look like Chuck Spoffard's right. Maybe I'd better let some younger man take over."

"Don't give up," Dave said. "Even if we did have some more grief tonight." He told about the riverfront prowler. "And me without even a gun on!"

Gilroy squinted thoughtfully. "Looks like Ogle really had the goods on 'em! They're scared we'll find it before they do. You and Buck better spend tomorrow takin' those joints to pieces. The shanty and the bar. We got to latch onto those guys before they run us clean outa the county."

"You talk like it's an organized gang."

"And why not? It took planning and organization, didn't it, to bushwhack Jake Slavin's stage? Look, boy. For a long time a smart gang of dust thieves have been operatin' over in the Leesburg basin. Every job they do shows timing; plus a foreknowledge of who's got a poke of gold dust and where. I figure there's a brain at the top who pulls every string. Pinky had the goods on 'em, some way, so they gunned him."

"Hold on!" Dave corrected. "Pinky was gunned to stop him from telling me who killed my brother."

"It doesn't seem to match up," Gilroy admitted. "But there's bound to be a connecting link somewhere. Go to bed now, boy; we'll take a crack at it tomorrow."

For Dave Harbison it was a day of frustration. He spent most of it helping Blanchard search a grove shanty and a riverfront bar. Nothing important was found at either place.

At noon he had lunch with Lisa. Afterward he walked her to the jail where she paid her daily visit to Court Grady.

The condemned man kissed her between the bars and then spoke with dignity and gratitude to Dave. "I haven't had a chance to thank you, young man." It was

Dave's first close sight of him since midmorning of four days ago, when Grady had stood on a scaffold in the yard.

By comparison the man looked relaxed now, and much younger in spite of his graying hair. A marked family resemblance to Lisa drew Dave to him. "To thank you," Grady repeated, "for saving my life."

It's not saved yet! Dave thought, but didn't say it. The same doom still hung over Court Grady and was only twenty-six days away.

"Looks like there's a tie-up between my case and yours, Mr. Grady. Did Lisa tell you?"

"She said the man who delayed my reprieve was caught searching the cabin of a man who was shot for saying he had proof about your brother's murder."

"You've got it in a nutshell," Dave said. "I'll leave you two together, Lisa. See you tonight at the hotel."

On the street he met Gilroy. The sheriff was back in harness today, gray and haggard and gun-weighted. "I'm on a still hunt for last night's prowler, Dave. You say he's pint-size and Buck says he wears Mexican spurs."

"The spurs raked me." Dave looked at his bruised finger.

"They clinked as he ran away, Buck says. Clinked like big loose iron rowels."

"Is Marvin Kane still in town?"

"Yep. And still wonderin' where Wes Gordon is. Kinda funny, Wes disappearin' like that."

Dave found Buck Blanchard at Pope's bar tossing down a whisky. As the deputy paid for it the bartender offered him a choice between two cards, one blue and one yellow. Dave looked on curiously as Buck chose the yellow one and dropped it into a slotted box at the end of the bar.

"A straw tally," he explained as he went out with Dave. "You get one vote with every drink. Blues are for Spoffard; yellows are for Gilroy."

"When do they count the votes?" Dave asked.

"Three weeks from Saturday night," Blanchard said. "Chuck Spoffard himself cooked up the idea. He's a spender. Every time he stands treat the other guy's a cinch to vote for him."

The two deputies went on to the riverfront and spent a fruitless afternoon there. Gilroy's luck was no better. At sun-down the three met at the hotel for supper. Dave looked about for Lisa but the girl didn't appear. "She had us send a snack up to her room," a waitress said.

Later Dave knocked on her door. Again he found Lisa making notes from old newspapers.

"I'm halfway through 1880," she reported. "Shall I read you what I've found?"

"Go ahead." Dave made himself comfortable with a cigarette.

Lisa opened a notebook and read:

#10 June 8 1879
Marvin Kane left for his ranch yesterday, after a week in town.

#11 Aug 10 1879
Laura Kane is spending a few days at the Kane cottage on St. Charles Street. She drove in alone from the ranch.

#12 Oct 5 1879
The Kaybar crew is out on fall roundup with Wes Gordon in charge.

#13 Oct 12 1879
Marvin Kane fell down the stairs while leaving Tony Sebastian's place Saturday night. Doctor Flint is treating his bruises.

#14 Oct 19 1879
Word comes from Haley that Gregg Harbison, who used to ride for the Kaybar, has purchased a placer claim on Wood River and is busy working it.

"That's all I found in the '79 volume," Lisa said.

Clearly it showed a rift between the Kanes. When one of them came to town, the other stayed out on the ranch. "He must've been drunk when he fell down those stairs. Didn't even go out on his own roundup." Dave looked again at item 14. After that, he reasoned, anyone up here would know right where to find Gregg.

"This is what I found in the first half of 1880." Lisa continued reading:

#15 Feb 16 1880
The Bal Masque at Shoup's Hall was a big

success. Chuck Spoffard, as Jim Bridger, and Alcinda Mulkey, as Sacajawea, won the costume prizes. When you get back to the Kaybar, Chuck, tell the Kanes we missed them.

#16 Apr 22 1880
Word comes from the Kaybar that Laura Kane has left Marvin. He returned home after a long spree in town to find her gone. One of the ranch hands drove her to Blackfoot, end of the UN rails. She boarded a train there for an unknown destination. We're not shedding very many tears for you, Marvin.

#17 May 6 1880
Chuck Spoffard, popular Lemhi Valley cowboy, has quit the Kaybar and gone to Denver.

#18 May 19 1880
Returning from a trip upvalley we stopped overnight at the Kaybar. Found no one there but the cook, Packy Blue. The crew, except for Kane himself, was off on roundup. The place seemed right dreary without Laura. No word from her, Packy said. Marv, we gathered, was off drowning his sorrow somewhere.

#19 June 1 1880
Shocking news from Hailey about Gregg Harbison, formerly of the Kaybar. While working his placer claim Gregg was sniped from the willows by an

unknown rifleman. He'd been dead several days when found. No clues. No known motive.

Dave's face was taut when Lisa looked up at him. "I spent eight months down there trying to turn up something."

"I have three more notations, Dave." The girl resumed reading:

#20 July 6 1880
Chuck Spoffard has returned from Denver where Dame Fortune smiled on him. Chuck spent three weeks on Holladay Street there and he says every card fell just right. He'll invest his stake, he says, in a good stock ranch right here in Lemhi County. You couldn't do better, Chuck.

#21 July 22 1880
All his friends will be glad to know that Chuck Spoffard, fortune's darling, has purchased the Box Q ranch up the Salmon River. And before we could stop batting our eyes on that one, he bowled us over with another. He'll run for sheriff in the fall election.

#22 July 28 1880
It's a season of wonders and the last one restores our faith in humankind. One of our oldest friends, to whom we now offer humble apology for certain sharp words aimed in his direction, is his old sober self again.

"That's as far as I've read." Lisa handed the notebook to Dave.

"So he swore off two years ago!" Dave brooded. "And according to Booth he's stuck to it."

"Losing Laura," Lisa supposed, "shocked him to his senses."

Dave looked at the notes and certain dates there impressed him sharply. Kane's reform had begun at about the time of Gregg Harbison's death. At about that same time Spoffard had made a trip to Denver — a journey from which he'd returned with a cash fortune. And at about that same season Marvin Kane had begun riding an *LD* horse.

"I better keep my fingers crossed, Lisa, till I have a talk with two men."

"Which two?"

"Couple of ex-Kaybar men. Pres Werner who they say is now tending bar at Shoup. And Packy Blue who's running a hash house at Leesburg."

An insistent knock took Dave to the door. Buck Blanchard stood in the hall with a grimness on his broad fleshy face. "Gilroy wants to see you right away, Dave. Some more grief just came in."

Dave followed him to the sheriff's room. Gilroy had a harassed look and was talking with a lanky, rock-scarred man in miner's boots.

"He's just up from Shoup," the sheriff told his deputies. "A hold-up and a killing down there. Three masked men. Two of 'em might be Brushy-Chin and Budlong."

"What did they do?"

"They gunned the manager of the Kentuck mine and cleaned out his safe."

Buck Blanchard took a hitch at his gunbelt. "You want Dave and me to ride down there?"

"First thing in the morning," Gilroy said.

CHAPTER
TWELVE

At sunup they were on their way. The trail led north out of Salmon City down the wide, tumbling river, with the Bitterroots on the right and the Salmon River Mountains on the left. Dave rode a roan ranch pony and Blanchard rode a powerful bay to match his size. This was exactly the path which, long ago, had been taken by two other venturesome men. Laura Kane, at an early breakfast with Dave and Lisa, had spoken of them; two men named Lewis and Clark who'd trailed by here searching for a passage to the westward sea.

There'd been no towns in those days, no ranches, no mines, no Idaho Territory, not even a wilderness trapper.

For a heavy man Buck Blanchard balanced gracefully in his saddle, cupping hands over a cigarette as he set the pace at a jog. Each cantle had a blanket roll back of it and each scabbard had a rifle. "It's forty miles, pardner. Take us ten hours; but the boats make it in seven."

Dave looked at the spray-flecked rapids and gave a shiver. "Not for me, Buck. I'll go broncback every time."

The mountains pinched closer with every downriver mile. By ten o'clock the valley became a canyon. The river here was a millrace of leaping white water. Buck twisted in the saddle to point upstream. "Here she comes, boy! And she'll pass us like we're standin' still."

They did stand still to watch the scow go by. Dave gaped in amazement as a forty-foot flatboat with a crew of two, laden with bags and crates, came plunging down the rapids. The thing had long pole sweeps, fore and aft, and the sweeps had six-foot blades. There was a raised platform at the center to give the pilot a better view of whatever treacherous hazards lay ahead.

Quickly the strange craft was opposite Dave. Blanchard waved and shouted to the crew. "Hi there, Eli! Ride her handsome, Jim!" But the crew, busy at the sweeps and with eyes on the lookout for upthrust rocks, had no time for greetings. On they went, weaving precariously to miss first one hazard then another. "She carries eight tons," Buck said. "But only once. This is the river of no return."

Presently the scow disappeared beyond a bend downcanyon. Dave and Buck jogged on.

Where Boyle Creek came in the canyon widened briefly to a valley and the deputies stopped at a small ranch there. A campaign poster tacked on the gate said: SPOFFARD FOR SHERIFF.

Tom Boyle fed them and grained their horses. Then the deputies pressed on. There was a stretch of slow deep water, then rapids again. A mule train passed them, heading upriver with sacked ore.

"It's from the Fourth of July mine," Buck said. "There's pay rock all the way from here to Shoup."

In early afternoon, where a fork from the north came in, the main river turned due west. The place had a supply store, a saloon and a few cabins. "Right here," Buck said, "is where we quit the Lewis and Clark trail. We go on down the main river and those fellas headed up North Fork."

"Is it shorter that way?" Dave suggested.

"Nope. It's longer. The way I heard it, Lewis and Clark had Indians with 'em: an old Indian named Toby and a gal named Sacajawea. Right here Toby told 'em they'd run into grief if they kept on down the main Salmon. Right below Shoup they'd get trapped in a narrow, fastwater gorge where even a boat can't go through; and if it went part way through it'd never get back. So Toby took 'em up North Fork and on over Lolo Pass."

The deputies rode on. And fifteen miles below North Fork, in late afternoon, they came to Shoup. It was a new gold town with a log hotel, two stores, a livery barn and a cluster of hillside cabins. Eli Suydam's freight scow had arrived and was being unloaded. Tomorrow it would be wrecked and the lumber used for cabins, the scow crew trailing back to Salmon City by wagon.

Again Dave saw a Spoffard-for-Sheriff poster.

"You put up the broncs and get us a room," Buck said, "while I check at the Kentuck mine."

Dave offsaddled at the livery stable, then carried both blanket rolls to the Westfall Hotel. A bar off the lobby had a big beet-faced tender back of it. Was he Pres Werner?

Dave was impatient to find out. He signed his own name and Blanchard's on the book and was given a room. The room's double bed sagged at the middle. Dave grimaced at the thought of sharing it with a man of Blanchard's bulk. Right now he must see Werner.

Customers at the bar were all miners. Dave stood apart from them and ordered beer. "You're Pres Werner?" he asked the brawny man who served him.

"That's me." The man looked at his customer's badge. "You're ridin' for Gilroy? That was a rum business at the Kentuck, night before last."

Dave nodded. "Buck Blanchard's up there getting the dope on it."

"Likely it's the same gang that's been raidin' placer claims over around Leesburg. They're dust-grabbers, mostly. Only this time they cleaned cash out of a safe."

"Know which way they went?"

"Nope. It was night time and their tracks stop in the river."

Dave sipped his beer, then asked casually, "By the way, didn't you use to work for the Kaybar ranch?"

"Yep, a right good outfit, the Kaybar. You acquainted there?"

"I knew a Kaybar rider named Harbison. Remember him?"

"Gregg Harbison? Sure I do."

"Remember the time he got bucked off a horse?"

Clearly the question puzzled Werner. "You must have him mixed up with someone else, neighbor. Gregg

Harbison was a top rider. If he ever got pitched off a horse, I never heard about it."

It hung a lie on Wes Gordon. Gordon who'd tried to steer Dave away from Werner! Just why, Dave wondered, did Gordon want him to stop asking about a certain punch in the jaw, four years ago at the Kaybar bunkhouse?

"You ribbed Gregg about something," Dave suggested, "and he took a swing at you. It was in the paper, remember?"

The barman's eyes narrowed and his beet face turned a shade redder. "Look, mister. You're gettin' kinda personal, ain'tcha? Who the hell *are* you, anyway?"

"Harbison's my name," Dave said. "Gregg was my brother and I want to know who killed him."

"Yeh? I heard about him gettin' shot but what's that got to to do with the Kaybar? It happened a long time after Gregg left there and a five-day ride away."

Dave admitted it. "But what did you say to him that made him sore?"

Pres Werner, who'd been friendly at the outset, all at once became cautious and hostile. He looked warily both ways along the bar. Then he leaned across it and lowered his voice. "If he took a swing at me, I don't remember it. And if you ask any more damnfool questions, I'll throw a punch myself. At you, mister. Right on the button. That beer'll be two-bits. You can pay me and get out."

"It's a cold trail," Buck Blanchard reported at supper. "Nobody saw 'em but the mine manager. They poked

122

guns into his ribs and made him open the safe. Soon as they cleaned it out they shot him. He only lived long enough to say they were three masked men, two tall and one short."

"Laura Kane has a mine down here," Dave remembered. "I'd like to see the man who runs it for her."

"It's the Bluebird. Jack Kelly's bossin' it and there he is now." Buck pointed to a shaggy, leather-coated man at another table.

Later Dave accosted him in the hotel office. "Mr. Kelly? I'm a friend of Laura Kane. You must've known her uncle. And maybe she talked to him a few times about why she left the Kaybar ranch. Did he ever pass it along to you?"

"Not to me," Kelly said. "But maybe to Ed Bellamy. I only took over a couple of months ago. Bellamy was mine foreman before that. He quit and started mining for himself up Arnett Creek. Just above Leesburg. You can look Ed up any time you go through there."

"I'll do that. Thanks."

Rejoining Blanchard, Dave found him in alert talk with a local corral hand who'd just returned from a grouse hunt. "They were headin' up Pine Creek, did you say, Lew?"

"Yep. I was a long way off and couldn't see 'em good. Three of 'em, two tall and one short. Two had horses and one rode a mule."

Buck turned grimly to Dave. "They might be the guys we want. We better take out after 'em, bright and early."

★ ★ ★

123

Dave hadn't been in bed with Buck five minutes before he realized they weren't alone. The fat man was already asleep and didn't seem to mind. *Maybe he's used to it; but I'm not!* The instant he was sure what the little crawling invaders were, Dave slipped out of bed. He dressed in the dark, groped for his saddle roll and went outside. It was cold out here, sleeping under a pine tree.

At daybreak he was up shivering and the hotel cook gave him breakfast. By the time he'd saddled the horses Buck was also ready to go. The river at Shoup had no bridge. "There's a place we can ford," Buck said, "a little way below here."

The crossing was stirrup deep and the water was icy on Dave's shins. They emerged chilled and dripping on the far bank. There a bridle trail led them downriver to the mouth of Pine Creek.

"If a boat ever gets below here she's a goner." Blanchard pointed downriver to a rock cliff rising sheer from the water. "The Indians put some picture writing on that cliff. Folks say it means, 'Who goes below here will never come back.'"

Dave nodded. "Laura Kane told me about it. Where the heck does it go, anyway?"

"Runs into the Snake, couple of hundred miles below here near the Oregon line."

They left the plunging Salmon and turned up the riffles of Pine Creek. If the grouse hunter's tip was worth anything, the Kentuck mine raiders had escaped this way. "Two broncs and a mule," Buck muttered.

Many pack trains had gone this way, so prints along the gravel creek bank meant little. "It's the regular freighting trail between Shoup and Leesburg," Buck said. "If those raiders took it I don't think they'd ride openly into Leesburg. The mine folks over there are plenty mad at dust robbers. There was some rope talk, last time I went through."

The big deputy rode slowly, eyes on the gravelly ground. And soon his strategy was clear to Dave. If the outlaws had taken this route, they'd leave it before getting too close to the placer settlements; and when they left it to veer off into virgin forest, riding two horses and a mule, their sign would show in the gravel.

Dave took one side of the beaten trail and Buck the other. The route steepened as they advanced, between slopes thickly wooded with lodgepole pine. After pushing on for an hour more they came to slash and a heap of sawdust where a lumber mill had once operated. "Right about here's where Lew saw 'em," Buck said.

Dave continued on, keeping in line with Blanchard, each man alert for turn-off sign. Dead ahead Dave saw a high timbered cone. "Do we go to the right of it, or to the left, Buck?"

"The pack trail goes to the left of it," Buck said. "It crosses a saddle at the head of Moose Creek, then cuts over another little divide to the head of Nappias. Couple of miles down Nappias Creek it comes to Leesburg."

"Anybody live on Moose Creek?"

"Yep. Right at the top of Moose there's some placer diggings and a dozen cabins."

"So to keep out of sight the raiders would have to go some other way?"

"That's what I'm countin' on," Buck said.

As they drew near the high timbered cone, the pack trail swerved to skirt it on the left. Hoofmarks angling the other way were so dim that Dave would have overlooked them. But Buck didn't. "Here's where they turned off, pardner." The big man dismounted to follow the prints afoot, bending low to see every tiny scar on the gravel.

"Not more'n a day old," he concluded. "Two broncs and a mule."

"How can you tell?" Dave wondered.

"Been trackin' all my life," Buck said.

The tracking demonstration he gave during the next few hours amazed Dave. Most of the way the ground was covered with pine needles. Faint game paths crossed it here and there. They saw bear sign and deer sign and elk sign. Grass was sparse and the soil, wherever it was exposed, was gravelly clay. The density of the forest filtered the sunlight and left them in a gray gloom. Occasionally they came to a tangle of windfalls. But always some scar or print or crushed stick told Buck which way to go.

Their route was detouring to the right of the high timbered cone. "What do they call it, Buck?"

"Haystack Mountain," Blanchard said; and with a start Dave knew he'd heard the name before.

Presently he remembered. Court Grady's alibi witness! A small, gold-toothed man on a buckskin horse, according to Grady, had asked him the way to Haystack Mountain. No one had ever been able to find that witness, and a jury had concluded he didn't exist.

"Who lives up this way, Buck?"

"Nobody, far as I know. It's a lonesome, empty neck of the woods. A right good hideout country, I'd say."

Aspen trees began showing among the pines, and occasionally a tall spired fir with short, down-slanting limbs.

A dead log barred the way and Buck said: "They stopped at this windfall. Stayed long enough to smoke five-six cigarettes. They tied the mule to that sapling. Didn't tie the horses at all; left the reins hangin'." Buck picked up a scrap of powder-blackened rag. "One of 'em cleaned his gun."

"Maybe they had a grub kit and stopped here to eat," Dave said. But any food crumbs would have been carried away by chipmunks.

Blanchard leaned his bulk across the windfall to look behind it. "Here's somethin' they dropped, pardner." He picked up an octagonal disk about the size of a half dollar. A man fishing a match from his pocket could have drawn the thing out by accident. "Know what it is?"

"If it was a circle," Dave said, "I'd call it a poker chip."

"You could cash this one," Buck said, "for a dollar at Tony Sebastian's. He's got the only joint in Idaho where they use eight-sided chips."

"Which proves what?"

"Not a thing," Blanchard admitted, "except that one of these birds bought chips at Tony's, one time. Lots of guys've done that, includin' myself."

They resumed the tracking, each man afoot and leading his horse. The route climbed steeply till they found themselves on a minor divide due west of Haystack Mountain.

Here Buck found sign which startled him. "A guy was waitin' for them here. They joined him and kept on going."

The going dipped downward toward the head of another small creek. "They call it Camp Creek," Buck said. "Look, pardner! This fourth jigger had a mule too. Makes two mules and two broncs."

Dave himself could see that much, a muleshoe being smaller and narrower than a horseshoe. "So if we catch up with 'em, Buck, it'll be a four-to-two fight."

They dropped into a ravine at the head of a small water run. The ravine was overgrown with gooseberry briers. "This crik flows into the Nappias at Leesburg," Buck said. "Looks like those guys headed for Leesburg after all; only they went in there by the back door."

"How far is it?"

"From here it's only about four miles. Get down, Dave! We're covered!" Buck whipped out his gun, dropping flat on the ground behind a log.

Dave dropped his reins and hit the dirt beside him. "What did you see, Buck?"

"Four rifle barrels," Buck said, "pointin' at us from a brier patch."

Back of them, their tired mounts stood with drooped heads and dangling reins. The rifles were still in the saddle scabbards. "We should've kept our mitts on 'em," Buck muttered.

Prone behind the log they were too low to see the brier patch with its four hostile rifles. "I'll wriggle back and get ours," Buck decided. "You stay here, pardner."

The big man crawled back toward the horses. As he reached his own he got to his knees and stretched an arm upward toward his saddle scabbard. It put his hand high enough to be seen over the briers and four rifle shots rang out. Bullets whipped through the brush and a horse reared, snorting from the pain of a hit. Buck flattened out of sight. "Keep low, Dave!" he shouted.

His voice drew a second volley from the briers. Again a horse snorted, reared, fell squealing to its fore knees and then went on down. At the log Dave raised himself till his eyes cleared the briers. He saw sunlight glinting on steel, aimed his six-gun that way and fired four fast shots.

The range was too long for short guns. A volley from rifles spat back at him. Dave ducked behind his log to reload. He waited a breathless minute but no more shots came.

Then Blanchard appeared beside him with two saddle guns, his own and Dave's. "They got our broncs," he reported glumly.

They crouched there with cocked guns, expecting to be be attacked. But nothing happened. The forest gave no sound except a low murmur from the creeklet.

129

"Maybe they ran for it," Dave said. "For all they know we're just the advance guard of a posse."

"Let's take a look."

They crawled over the log and moved warily forward, eyes and ears alert. No challenge came from the briers. When they searched there they found twelve empty rifle shells and a smell of burned powder. Nothing more.

"Looks like the fight's over," Buck concluded. "Them with broncs and us on foot, we can't very well chase 'em. And if we did we'd get beaned from the next brier patch."

He went back to the horses and Dave heard two shots. "They were still kicking," he explained as Dave joined him, "so I stopped their misery."

They took the gear from the dead horses, shouldered it and began trudging down Camp Creek. "How far did you say, Buck?"

"To Leesburg? Far enough," Blanchard growled, bending under the weight of his saddle. "Be dark when we get there." His fleshy, sweat-streaked face took a sardonic grin. "How do yuh like sheriffin' by this time, pardner?"

"I'd rather herd cattle, Buck. Or even sheep."

CHAPTER
THIRTEEN

It was the longest four miles, and the heaviest saddle, that Dave had ever known. With Blanchard he staggered boneweary into Leesburg just after nightfall. The camp's constable spotted them and came up curiously. "You look all stove up, Buck. How come you're on foot?"

While Blanchard explained, Dave went to a sprawling log hotel and took a room with two beds in it. It was clean and the beds had fresh sheets. After he'd washed, the hotel woman gave Dave supper. Then he went out to look for Blanchard.

The place had only one street but it was nearly a mile long. It ran parallel to Nappias Creek with blocky log houses lining it. In the camp's heyday there'd been four saloons but only one was operating now. All stores but one were boarded up and about half the cabins were vacant. At this hour there was no light except starlight and a few lamplit windows. And little sound other than the strumming of a miner's guitar and a swish of riffles from the creek. Of the few people Dave saw, about half were Chinese. When a placer camp began to play out, he'd been told, Chinese were likely to move in and take over the worn-out claims.

Dave found Buck Blanchard at the livery stable. He and the constable were arranging for horses. "I'll round up a posse for you, Buck," the constable promised. "In the mornin' you can get an early start and try trackin' them raiders. Them dustrobbers'll steal us outa house and home, unless we run 'em down."

"Where's Packy Blue's restaurant?" Dave asked.

"Come along," Buck said. "I'd as lief eat there as anywhere." He took Dave up the street to a sign that said,

BLUE'S BEANERY

They went in and a chunky man with a hairless head served them. "Beef or mutton, Buck?"

"Beef and plenty of it," Buck said.

"Just coffee for me," Dave added.

While they waited Blanchard remarked, "It ain't what it used to be, this camp."

"How old is it?"

"Sixteen years. Five Confederate vets came out here in '66 and struck it rich. Eli Mulkey was one of 'em. They laid out this camp and named it after General Lee. By the fall of '69 it had three thousand people."

Packy Blue came in with Buck's supper and Dave spoke to him. "Didn't you use to cook for the Kaybar ranch?"

"Yeh, and I was a sight better off there than I am here."

"Why did you quit?"

132

Packy shrugged. "Seemed like the place was goin' to pot. Wasn't the same after the missus left. What with the boss crocked half the time I just didn't cotton to that job any more."

"They say he reformed, right after you left."

The man nodded. "But I was there when he tied on the last one. The crew was off on spring roundup, all but me and the boss. It was about three weeks after the missus quit us. The boss took it plenty hard."

"So he went to town on a binge?"

"Usually he did," Blue remembered, "but not that time. I recollect Booth of the newspaper stoppin' by and askin' where he was. It was none of his damn business so I didn't tell him."

"That was two years ago," Dave coaxed, "so no harm in tellin' me now."

"Reckon not," Packy Blue agreed. "Fact is he strapped a sackful of liquor back of his saddle and rode off to our south line camp. Holed up there on a solo bender for ten days. Must've been a beaut!" Packy grinned and added reminiscently: "Funny thing is, it cured him. Came back and swore off for keeps."

"Came back riding a strange brand, didn't he?"

The ex-Kaybar cook blinked with a mild surprise. "Come to think of it, I believe he did. Told me he'd sobered up to find his horse had strayed off and left him afoot. So he walked to the road and flagged down some immigrant outfit trailin' by. Bought a bronc from 'em and rode home. How about a slab of pie, mister?"

"Make it gooseberry," Dave said.

When the man went for it Blanchard cocked a curious eye. "What are you tryin' to dig up, fella?"

"I'm not sure," Dave brooded. He remembered it was at that same south line camp that Gregg Harbison had spent his last night in Lemhi County. Could there be a connection? "Ask me again, Buck, after I've talked to Ed Bellamy. The man who used to foreman the Bluebird mine at Shoup. He's got a diggings of his own now, here at Leesburg."

"It's a short shake up Arnett Creek," Buck said. "Okay. You can look him up tomorrow while I take that posse up Camp Creek. There'll be plenty of us without you goin' along. If I'm not back in a day or two, you can ride the Yellow-jacket stage down to Salmon."

A posse of miners, led by Blanchard, had already left camp when Dave finished breakfast in the morning. Arnett Creek came in near the south end of the street and a ten-minute walk up it brought Dave to Ed Bellamy's claim.

Bellamy was building a brush dam to divert water into his sluice ditch. He was a wiry little man with graying hair. "I'm a friend of Laura Kane," Dave said. "You worked for her uncle, I understand."

"That's right." The miner wore gum boots and stood ankle deep in the creek. "Foremanned for him the last coupla years before he died."

"Did his niece ever go down to Shoup to see him?"

"Twice." Bellamy tamped tobacco into his pipe. "Came down to ask his advice. And from what he told me she sure needed it."

134

"What about?"

The miner waded ashore. "A man needs warmin' up after messin' around in this creek. Come join me in a cup of coffee."

Dave followed him to a cabin. The stove had a pot on it and Bellamy poured two cups. "She had husband trouble," he said. "Seems like she was married to some bottle hound and was tryin' to make up her mind what to do."

"What did her uncle advise?"

" 'If it happens again,' he told her, 'pack up and leave.' "

"If what happened again?"

"I'm not sure," Bellamy said. "But from what the boss told me it went something like this. Her husband had a big ranch. Coupla years before the bust-up, a sharp-looking cowboy came by and took a job. Worked there about six months. When he left, everybody on the outfit knew why."

"Yeh? Why did he leave?"

"Seems like he had the bad luck to fall in love with the boss's wife. He didn't say anything or do anything he oughtn't to. But it was plain enough to everybody on the ranch. One of the crew kidded him about it and got socked on the beezer. So soon as the fall roundup was over he quit and lit out for another range."

"You mean he quit just to stop the talk?"

"That's the way I get it."

"What about Laura? How well did she like this cowboy?"

"All I know is what she told her uncle, nearly a year later when she began asking his advice. She said both she and her husband knew why this cowboy left. If the husband was jealous, he hid it till after the cowboy pulled out. Then Laura said he began imagining things. Once he found her writing a letter and he asked if she was writing to the cowboy. She said no, it was to her uncle at Shoup. He asked to see the letter and it made her mad. She locked him out of her room so he went off and got drunk."

"This went on for a year?" Dave prompted.

"For a year and a half, all told. Each time it got worse. A suspicious question which she'd take as an insult. Then he'd go to town or to some line camp and stay drunk for a week."

"So she asked her uncle what to do," Dave summed up. "He told her to pack up and leave."

"Which she did. And she didn't tell her husband where. He didn't know where she'd gone till he got a notice from a California court telling him she was there, and setting a date for a divorce hearing."

"How do you know that?"

"Laura wrote her uncle from California. She said the notice had brought a letter of apology from her husband, begging her to come back and swearing he'd never take another drink."

"Which he never has," Dave said.

He left Bellamy and walked back down Arnett Creek. A question buzzed under his hat and it had to be answered. Just what had gone on in the jealous mind

136

of Marvin Kane on the day he'd come home to find Laura gone? Gone where? To join Gregg Harbison?

She hadn't, of course. She'd gone to Blackfoot by buckboard and from there by train to California. She'd never again seen Gregg since he'd quit the ranch, in the fall of '78.

But twenty months later, when without note of explanation Laura had left there herself, in Kane's mind it might have been to join Gregg at Hailey. An insanely jealous husband could easily suspect that. If so, had he gone there himself on a mission of revenge?

Packy Blue thought he'd gone to a line camp on a ten-day bender. But the same ten days could have been used for a round trip ride to Hailey. A fast ride on which he might founder his mount, forcing him to pick up another one at the nearest ranch!

Dave turned into Leesburg's long, winding street, his mind wrestling pro and con with the case against Marvin Kane. The shooting of Gregg Harbison had occurred at about that time. For Kane there'd been both motive and opportunity. Maybe he'd shot Gregg on sight, then gone to the cabin to confront Laura. Finding that she wasn't there, and that she'd never been there, and that the cabin didn't even hold a letter from her . . . all that could shock Kane into an agony of remorse. A shock which would make him swear off liquor and write an humble apology to Laura, when at last a court notice gave him her address.

A poster tacked on a log wall caught Dave's eye. SPOFFARD FOR SHERIFF. Others like it were in sight along the street.

It pulled Dave's thoughts away from Kane and pinned them on Spoffard. Spoffard and his trip to Denver in the spring of 1880! He could have gone by way of Hailey without losing more than a day or two. Which meant that he too had had a physical opportunity for the crime there.

Opportunity but no motive. As far as Dave knew, Gregg had never quarreled with Chuck Spoffard. Between them there'd been no competition or rivalry.

Yet a straw of fact reared up to challenge Dave. Upon leaving the Kaybar, Gregg had stopped overnight with Spoffard at the ranch's south line camp; the very camp which, a year and a half later, had according to Packy Blue been occupied for ten days by Marvin Kane.

Noon came and Dave made a point to eat at Packy's. Again he quizzed the ex-cook about Laura Kane's last days at the Kaybar, and about the rancher's reaction to her leaving.

"Just like I said, mister. He took it hard. Went on one last binge and stayed boiled for ten days. Purty soon after that I quit my job. Next I heard he was on the wagon."

"Does Wes Gordon know you're running this beanery?"

"Sure he does. Wes has been over here and et with me more'n once."

"He told me he doesn't know where you are; or where Pres Werner is. When we asked him again, he ducked out of town."

138

Blue rubbed his chin thoughtfully. "Might be he just don't like the idea of rakin' over old bones. One thing you can say for Wes Gordon; and Pres Werner too, far as that goes; they're both what you'd call plumb loyal to Kane and the Kaybar. If you start pinnin' 'em down about Kane's booze-fighting days, they're likely to duck." The cook finished with a grin, "Fact is, I'm surprised Pres Werner didn't take a poke at you."

"He almost did," Dave said.

The stage from Yellowjacket was due shortly and he decided to ride it to Salmon City. Waiting for it he went into the saloon for a beer. A knot of miners at the bar had their heads together. Their subdued talk stopped as Dave entered. He wondered why until he saw their eyes fixed furtively on his badge.

He'd caught the last few words of the talk. "The trap's all set!"

A man who'd spoken them had a guilty look. "A bear trap?" Dave asked him.

The group shifted uneasily. The bartender gave a hollow laugh. Then another man answered half under his breath, "No, a skunk trap."

Dave lingered there waiting for the stage. When he heard it come in he crossed to the hotel for his saddle and blanket roll. The stage, which was only a battered spring wagon with a canvas top, was at the livery barn changing horses as Dave approached it. And again he heard a knot of men break off a low-toned discussion. Again he caught the final words of it: "A skunk trap, Jase told him; but he didn't ketch on. And he's leavin' on the stage . . ."

"I was," Dave said, appearing suddenly among them. "But I've changed my mind. What is it you don't want me to ketch on about?"

"We was just foolin'," a man muttered. The others promptly scattered. The stage driver spoke to Dave. "Understand you're ridin' with me, mister. If you don't mind gettin' your teeth jolted out, climb on."

"I'll rent me a horse," Dave decided, "and go by saddle."

He hunted up the barn man and made arrangements to leave on a rented horse early in the morning. Then he moved about town with his eyes and ears open. "What's going on?" he asked Packy Blue.

But Packy, talkative enough on other matters, was mum on this one. It was the same at the store, the hotel and the livery barn.

At dusk the camp's constable, who'd gone out with Blanchard's posse, returned alone. "Them raiders are headed fer the Yellowjacket country, looks like. Buck and the boys are still after 'em."

"What's this about a skunk trap?" Dave questioned.

"I wouldn't know," the constable answered cautiously, then turned away with a shrug.

It was seven in the morning before Dave got the answer. On a rented saddle horse he took the road toward Salmon City. It crossed Nappias Creek at the north end of Leesburg and then climbed a wooded trail up Sawpit Creek toward a mountain notch.

As he approached a pine tree by the road, only two miles out of Leesburg, Dave's horse shied. Gliding shadows on the ground meant circling buzzards. Then

140

Dave saw another shadow. A gruesome one cast by a man's body hanging from a limb of the pine.

A lynching! A paper tacked on the tree had three words on it:

DUST PROWLERS, BEWARE

So this one had been caught in a trap last night, and hanged by starlight! A skunk trap, they'd called it.

They could spread a rumor, Dave reasoned, about some outlying cabin with a poke of dust in it; then wait in ambush for a thief. According to Ad Gilroy, for a long time these Leesburg Basin miners had suffered heavy losses. So they'd taken the law into their own hands.

The hanging man was sharp-featured and of small build. Dave stood at full height on his saddle and cut him down.

Not till the body hit the dust did he notice the spurs. They were Mexican spurs with big sharp rowels. Dave looked at a scratch on his own finger. Here, then, was the man who only three nights ago had prowled a riverfront barroom with a candle.

CHAPTER
FOURTEEN

When Sheriff Gilroy entered the International Hotel dining room at suppertime he saw Lisa at a table with Laura Kane. The girl's eyes had an anxious question and she didn't need to put it into words. A third of her respite had gone by; for this was the tenth day of a thirty-day reprieve. And that gallows tower still waited in the jailyard.

"Nothing new, Lisa," Gilroy reported wearily.

Laura asked, "Is Dave Harbison back yet?"

The sheriff shook his head. "Nor Buck Blanchard either. Accordin' to the Yellowjacket stage driver, they tracked those guys from Shoup to a brier patch just above Leesburg. Traded a few slugs with 'em, I hear."

Gilroy was about to move on when Laura Kane suggested cordially, "You look lonesome, Sheriff. Won't you join us?"

"Thanks." It was a table for four and when Gilroy sat down there was still an empty chair.

Another man came in and looked hopefully at it. He stopped a moment, but if anyone invited him to sit down it would have to be Laura Kane. She gave only a formal nod. Lisa's smiling, "Good evening, Mr. Kane," was echoed by Gilroy's hearty: "Hello, Marvin. When are you goin' back to the ranch?"

"First thing in the morning," Kane answered, and moved on to eat alone.

Lisa couldn't help feeling sorry for him. Her glance at Laura was almost reproachful.

They were nearly through supper when a woman who didn't belong here appeared in the dining room doorway. Her cheeks and lips were too red, her gown considerably too low-cut for this end of the street. Her eyes seemed frightened as they searched the room for Gilroy.

Then she came straight to him and spoke in a pitch of nervous excitement. "There's a man at Tony's place, Sheriff. He asked for me but I slipped down the backstairs."

Gilroy stood up. "Yeh? What did he want, Cherry?"

"He's Tracy Smith of Cheyenne. If he finds me . . ."

The sheriff broke in gruffly. "Begin at the start."

Laura Kane said quietly, "Won't you sit down?"

But Cherry of Sebastian's knew her place. Salmon City wouldn't approve of her sitting down with ladies like Lisa Grady and Laura Kane. She remained standing as she answered Gilroy. "Two years ago he killed a man while I was working at the Casino in Cheyenne. They were hunting all over town for him. He came to my room and asked me to hide him. Instead I told the police where he was and they gave him a life sentence. At the trial he said he'd kill me some day."

"You mean he escaped?"

Cherry looked nervously over her shoulder. "He just walked into Sebastian's and asked for me. He's waiting for me there."

"He's got a gun?"

"Yes, and he's a draw-fighter. They called him the fastest in Wyoming."

Ad Gilroy drooped his lips, shrugging. "Okay, Cherry. You stay out of sight while I go pick him up."

Laura Kane made a quick protest. "Not by yourself! You'll need help."

"The only help I've got," Gilroy said grimly, "are Buck Blanchard and Dave Harbison. They're both out of town." He left them abruptly and went out to the street.

Cherry stared after him. "He hasn't a chance," she murmured. "Not by himself; not with Tracy Smith."

Lisa, glancing about the room, saw many eyes on them. Ears had been wide open to catch Cherry's harassed plea. They all knew what it meant. Ad Gilroy, tired and old and only a few days out of a sick bed, was on his way to meet a draw-fighter from Wyoming.

"Won't someone please go with him?" Suddenly Laura Kane was on her feet and appealing to every man in the room. None of them was armed. But a lobby rack had a number of gun-belts hanging on it. "He'll be killed," Laura said urgently, "if he fights that man alone." Everyone knew that Ad Gilroy was gun-slow; he'd never pretended to be anything else. The people of Lemhi County had made him sheriff simply because they liked and trusted him. "Won't someone please help him?" Laura begged.

144

With one exception, every man in the room kept his seat. That one got up and walked briskly out. As he passed by Lisa heard him say quietly, "Of course, Laura."

She saw him take his gunbelt from the lobby rack, buckle it on and go outside.

After half a minute of tense stillness, nearly everyone else in the hotel surged out after him. They bunched on the porch and sidewalk, looking down Main toward a two-story brick a block west. Tony's place was on the upper floor. Nearly there now, walking down the middle of the street, was Ad Gilroy.

Racing after him was Marvin Kane. "Wait for me, Sheriff!" Lisa and Laura heard the shout as they emerged on the hotel porch.

Gilroy stopped, turned, waited for him. The two held a brief colloquy, then moved on toward Sebastian's. Watching from a distance, Lisa caught a single breathless word from Laura. "Don't!" It could only mean, "Don't go, Marvin!"

Lisa took the older woman's hand, found it cold and trembling. If Marv Kane met death in the next minute it would be because a woman he'd lost had sent him to it. And now she wished she hadn't. A dread in her eyes said, "Come back!"

They all saw Kane and Gilroy arrive at Sebastian's hitchrack. A single saddle horse was tied there. A horse with a strange brand, probably, because Kane and Gilroy gave it a close inspection, pausing there a minute to discuss it. Tracy Smith's mount, no doubt.

By this time customers from all three of the Main Street bars had poured out on the walks. Some rumor of a killer at Tony's place must have spread swiftly, for all groups gazed intently that way.

They saw Kane and Gilroy leave the hitchrack and cross the walk. Elbow to elbow they disappeared upstairs leading to the gambling parlors of Tony Sebastian.

Lisa felt Laura Kane's fingernails dig into the flesh of her hand. In the tense silence which ruled the street she could almost hear the beating of her own heart.

A minute went by. Gilroy and Kane must be facing the man now. Lisa hoped desperately he'd surrender without a fight.

But he didn't. Open upper windows gave out the sound of two shots. They came clearly from Sebastian's bar. Two gunshots and then silence.

Had Gilroy and Kane fired the shots? Or had they received them from Tracy Smith?

A moment later everyone knew. A man came down the stairs and out on the walk. He was neither Kane nor Gilroy. It was the twilight hour and in the fading light Lisa could see only that he was a man with a holstered gun. He stepped quickly to his horse, untied it, raised a foot to a stirrup.

A challenge stopped him. The nearest saloon was the Bit Bar and a man who come out of it was Chuck Spoffard.

"What's your hurry?"

Spoffard's sharp shout made Tracy Smith step away from his horse, giving himself elbow room for a draw.

The outlaw took a crouching stance as he faced Spoffard. The two were half a block apart. A hit by either at that range would need close shooting.

Lisa and fifty others watched from the hotel walk. They heard a second shout from Spoffard. Its tone was bold and confident. "I'm not sheriff yet. But I soon will be. So here I come, mister."

In the thinning twilight all of Salmon City looked on, as Chuck Spoffard advanced toward the stranger. His hands hung loose, graceful, ready. The man from Cheyenne hadn't moved. He still stood in a crouch a pace from his saddled mount. A draw-fighter, Cherry called him.

They were sixty yards apart; then fifty; then forty.

At thirty yards both men drew. The two shots blotted each other. Lisa covered her eyes for a moment; then opened them to see that it was Tracy Smith who'd gone down, arms hugging his stomach as he lay in the Main Street dust.

From an open upper window leaned Tony Sebastian. "He downed Gilroy," Tony yelled to the street. "And Kane too. But they ain't either of 'em hurt bad."

Lisa felt Laura's hand relax in her own. From the saloon block came a hubbub of cheering. A man yelled, "It was your party, Chuck!"

Another shouted: "You don't need to electioneer any more. Not after this. You've got it made, Chuck!"

Lisa could hardly doubt it. Nor could anyone else on the street. For under a test of fire it was Chuck Spoffard, and not Sheriff Gilroy, who had upheld the law in Lemhi County.

CHAPTER
FIFTEEN

Dave Harbison rode into Kingsbury's livery barn an hour after midnight. Every bone in his body ached. It was seventeen hours since he'd cut that hangbird down. There'd been no choice other than to take the dead man back to the Leesburg constable and spend the day trying to uncover the guilt of lynching.

A completely futile day. He'd had the feeling that half of Leesburg knew all about it; but no tongue would tell a tale. So after supper Dave had taken the stage road again, riding up Sawpit, over the hump and down Jesse Creek to Salmon City.

"You missed a right good show," the barn man chuckled.

"I've had all the shows I want," Dave said.

"This one was a lulu! Draw-fighter from Wyoming shot up Tony's place. Then Chuck Spoffard out-triggered him in the street."

Dave turned alertly. "What's that? Where was Gilroy?"

"Him and Marv Kane got batted down," the hostler said.

Bit by bit Dave dug the high points from him. Gilroy and Kane, he learned, had gone to Sebastian's to arrest a man named Smith. But from a window Smith had seen them coming and was ready. It was too early for much trade and so the place was empty except for Tony himself and one table of unarmed poker players. Covering them with a gun, Smith had posted himself in ambush just inside the door, waiting for Gilroy and Kane.

"Kane came in first and the man whanged him down with a gun barrel. Ad came in next and this Smith punched a gun in his ribs. He made Tony and the card players lay flat on the floor. Then he put Ad to sleep alongside Marv Kane."

Dave stared. "You mean there was no shooting?"

"None except two shots the man fired over their backs, to warn 'em what'd happen if they didn't keep layin' there. Then he went down to his bronc. He'd've got clean away except for Spoffard. Chuck came outa the Bit Bar and outgunned him."

"Where's Gilroy now?"

"They put him to bed. And Kane too. They'll wake up with headaches, that's all."

Dave crossed to the hotel. Chung was just closing the bar and he confirmed the liveryman's information. "The sheriff sleeps," Chung finished. "Best you do not disturb."

Dead on his feet, Dave went up to his own room and to bed. When he wakened it was midmorning. He dressed hurriedly, shaved, then stepped down the hall to Gilroy's room. No one was there. The bed had been slept in. Apparently the sheriff had gotten up and gone to his duties.

Dave knocked at Lisa's door and got no answer. In the lobby he was told she'd breakfasted two hours ago. Right now she was paying her regular morning visit at Court Grady's cell.

After eating Dave went over there himself. Gilroy was at his desk. He looked so abjectly unhappy that Dave put an extra accent of heartiness in his greeting. "Good morning, Sheriff."

"Nothin' good about it," Gilroy muttered. His head had two bumps now, one from Brushy-Chin and one from Tracy Smith.

"Is Blanchard back yet?"

"No. Didja find out who did that lynching?" Evidently the Yellowjacket stage driver had brought news of it to the county seat.

"It's a blind alley." Dave gave a report of his own adventures and then listened to Gilroy's account of the Tracy Smith affair. "Makes Chuck Spoffard top man in the sheriff's race," Gilroy concluded glumly. "The boys are countin' me out at every bar in town."

"Where's Kane?"

"He hit for the ranch, about an hour ago, headache and all."

Dave stood weighing his own suspicions of Kane. Should he discuss them with Gilroy? Then he remembered an inquiry he'd mailed to the *LD* ranch, in the Hailey area. Maybe he'd better wait for an answer before pointing a finger at Kane.

While he debated the matter, Lisa came in from the cell corridor. She'd been visiting with her father. Her small, delicate face showed the strain she'd been under.

150

He knew she was scoring every minute of these thirty days, of which eleven had already slipped by.

But now Dave saw an odd look of puzzlement in her eyes as she spoke to him. "Dad wants you to say that again, Dave — what you said when you came in."

"I asked if Blanchard was back," Dave remembered.

"No, it was before that. The very first thing you said."

"I came in and said 'Good morning, Sheriff.'"

"Say it again, Dave," the girl insisted. "Loud and hearty, so Dad can hear you."

With a confused smile, as though he were pampering a whim, Dave repeated the greeting. "Good morning, Sheriff."

"Come," Lisa said. "Both of you."

Mystified, Dave and Gilroy followed her to the cell room. Court Grady stood behind the bar with a strange alertness on his prison-pale face.

"Good morning, Sheriff!" he repeated, as though the words had a magic meaning. "When you said it that way, hale and hearty, I remembered where I'd heard it before."

Gilroy gaped at him. "People say it every day, Grady."

"I guess they do," the condemned man agreed. "A man said it to me, one time — and I never was a sheriff."

"When and where?" Dave asked him.

"In Virginia City, Montana," Grady told them. "It was in May of '79. I was on my way to Idaho and stopped overnight there."

151

Dave looked questioningly at Lisa and she nodded. "Dad came west on a steamboat up the Missouri River."

He naturally would, Dave admitted. For in 1879 the Utah Northern railroad, tapping Idaho from the south, hadn't been built. To arrive here that year an immigrant would be likely to travel up the Missouri to the end of navigation, and from there on by stage or saddle. His route would take him through Montana's most active gold town, Virginia City.

"I didn't know a soul there," Grady said. "Got up in the morning and started for the livery barn to saddle my horse. A man came along, looked me in the face and said, 'Good morning, Sheriff.'"

Dave pounced on it. "Someone mistook you for the Virginia City sheriff?"

"All I know is what I just told you. He said 'Good morning, Sheriff,' then kept on down the walk. I was heading the other way, in a hurry to get my horse and ride on."

"Don't you see what it means?" Lisa exclaimed eagerly.

"Means whoever was sheriff at Virginia City, in '79," Dave concluded, "looks something like your dad."

"But he doesn't!" The hope was short-lived as Ad Gilroy dashed it. "In '79, A. J. Edsall was sheriff at Virginia City. He still is. He's honest as daylight and one of my best friends. He's tall, dark, with a narrow face and thin black hair. Grady's three inches shorter, with blue eyes in a round face, and with thick light hair. They're opposite types."

Dave's face clouded and the same disappointment was on Lisa's. "You're sure of it?"

"Dead sure of it. I was over there to pick up a horse thief, one time. Edsall kept me overnight at his house. Folks over that way think a heap of him and they keep reelecting him every two years."

The hope snuffed out. Court Grady's memory, Dave thought, must have played him a trick. Three years was a long time to remember a casual sidewalk greeting.

He walked back to the hotel with Lisa. "For a minute I thought we had something," Dave said. "A long time ago they had a crooked sheriff at Virginia City named Plummer. The town turned out and hanged him, one day. But that was more than fifteen years ago."

The girl gave a sigh. "If they'd only had one like that *three* years ago! A man of Dad's build and coloring . . ."

"In that case," Dave said, "he could be the man who killed Whitey Parks, up the Lemhi. The Richmire couple could've thought he was Court Grady."

But it all ran into a stone wall because the Virginia City sheriff, both now and three years ago, was an honest man bearing no remote resemblance to Grady.

"I suppose," Lisa concluded, "that Dad is mixed up about the time and place. No wonder, after all he's been through!"

She went up to her room and Dave, looking across the street, saw a dusty Buck Blanchard dismount at the livery barn.

Promptly Dave joined him. "What luck, Buck?"

153

The big man grimaced wryly. "I rode twenty pounds of meat off; plus ten gallons of sweat. Outside of that I didn't have any luck at all."

"Where did the sign take you?"

"To where the Nappias hits Panther Creek. Right there those four dust-snatchers split; three rode west toward Yellow-jacket and the posse kept after 'em; the fourth man headed east toward Williams Creek Pass and I took off after him."

"He crossed the pass?"

"Yeh, and then came down Williams Creek to the Salmon River. He was forkin' a mule. Lost his sign in the river near the Box Q."

"Had any breakfast?"

Buck nodded. "At the Box Q. Stayed all night there. Chuck Spoffard showed up himself about bedtime; he told me about the ruckus at Sebastian's. Is Gilroy all right?"

"All except his feelings," Dave said.

"I hear you had a rope party at Leesburg."

"Yeh, and guess who. The little guy with the Mexican spurs; the one who prowled Pinky's bar with a candle."

They went to the sheriff's office and relaxed over cigarettes. "Somehow it all comes back to Pinky Ogle," Buck muttered. "He had something stashed away and they looked for it at his shanty, at his bar . . ."

"Maybe it was on him when he died!" Dave broke in thoughtfully. "What was done with his clothes, Buck?"

Blanchard went to a storage closet and came back with a boxful of garments. "It's what Pinky had on; we're holdin' it in case some of his kin show up."

Dave went through the pockets; he even slit the linings but could find nothing of interest.

A man passed along the walk and Buck called to him. "Hi, there; got a message for you, Whipple."

The cattle buyer looked in. "A message for me? Who from?"

"From Chuck Spoffard. He says that bid you made on his steers is no good. It's ten dollars a head under the market."

Whipple shrugged. "He can take it or leave it."

When he moved on Blanchard gazed quizzically after him. "He did the same thing at the Mulkey ranch; and at the Kaybar; and at Barrock Brothers. Bid ten dollars under the market and got turned down."

Buck went to the hotel for a bath and Dave drifted from bar to bar, from shop to shop, keeping his ears open and asking a few quiet questions. At Leesburg the lynched man had been identified as an ex-mucker named Fergie. Dave tried in vain to find someone in Salmon City who'd known Fergie.

After supper at the hotel he summed it up to Gilroy and Blanchard. "We know Fergie was tied up with the gold-dust raiders, because he was lynched for it. He was tied to Pinky Ogle because he prowled Pinky's bar for the same thing Brushy-Chin was hunting at Pinky's shack. Pinky called it proof about my brother's murder. And it was Brushy-Chin who delayed Grady's reprieve."

"Which puts it all in one package," Gilroy muttered.

Chung appeared at Dave's elbow. "The young lady sends for you, sir. She has something of importance."

Dave went up to Lisa's room. When he opened the door her face had a rich excitement. "Look what I've found, Dave!" She took him to a bound file of the Salmon City *Recorder* which was spread open on the bed.

"Thought you finished with 'em, Lisa."

"I did. I read clear up to this summer without finding anything worth showing you. But this morning Mr. Gilroy mentioned his friend Sheriff Edsall over in Montana. Remember?"

"That's right. An honest man who doesn't look a bit like your father."

"But when I thought about it," Lisa said, "the name Edsall seemed vaguely familiar. I'd read it somewhere recently — and it had to be in one of Mr. Booth's old news files. Dad came through Virginia City in May of '79. So I asked Mr. Booth to bring me the 1879 volume again. He did. I turned to May. And found this!"

The file was open to an issue dated in May three years ago. Lisa put her finger on a short news item and Dave read it aloud.

Word comes to us from across the Montana border that A. J. Edsall, popular and efficient sheriff of Madison County, was recently pitched from a horse and suffered three broken ribs. The *Recorder* wishes him a speedy recovery.

"He'd be laid up at least a month, wouldn't he, Dave?"

156

"Twice that," Dave thought, "and when a sheriff goes to bed for that long somebody has to pick up his badge. They'd appoint a temporary acting sheriff, likely."

"Since it happened in May of '79, it could be the man someone mistook for Dad!"

"It sure could, Lisa. Which means he looks like your dad. He'd serve a few months while Edsall was laid up, then go back to his regular job. By now he could be a stock hand or a blacksmith or even an outlaw. I've got to find him; and stand him in front of the Richmires."

"If you only could!" The girl's eyes beseeched him.

"I can if he's still in Virginia City."

"How far is it?"

"About a hundred and sixty miles, I'd say. A stage to Red Rock, a train to Dillon, then a stage to Virginia City."

The round trip might take nearly a week. But it was well worth it. If Grady had been mistaken for the man three years ago, the same mistake could have been made a few months ago by the Richmires.

"When will you start?" Lisa asked urgently.

"Right after you kiss me good-bye."

Without waiting, Dave kissed her lips. For a moment he held her in his arms, then stood away, laughing at her astonished face. "Go down and tell Gilroy. Ask him to write me a note of introduction to Edsall. And book a seat for me on Jake Salvin's stage."

CHAPTER
SIXTEEN

Promptly at seven in the morning Jake Slavin whipped his horses to a trot, making dust out of town. Again Dave Harbison chose the high seat beside him. "Seems like I've seen you before," Jake grinned. "Hope we have better luck this time."

Dave had a six-gun but no rifle. If he should need a saddle gun, Sheriff Edsall would furnish him one. In his wallet was a letter to Edsall from Gilroy.

Seven miles upvalley they passed the Mulkey gate. And a mile beyond that gate the stage slowed to cross a small creek coming in from the other side. Dave looked up its course, to the step, timbered fastness of the Bitterroot range, and remembered that this was Geerston Creek.

A stray string of thought touched his mind. Something about a bear hunt up Geerston Creek. A five-man party organized by Chuck Spoffard. They'd postponed it a month, Dave remembered. A month which happened to coincide with Court Grady's reprieve.

The stage rumbled on. A mile beyond Geerston Creek Dave saw Grady's little ranch, deserted now, its sheds bunched lonely and forlorn by the Lemhi Creek willows. "They put Grady's livestock in Mrs. Mulkey's pasture for the time being," Slavin remarked. "There've been a couple of offers to buy Grady out, I hear, but that girl of his says no. She just won't give up hope of her old man going back there. Reckon there's any chance?"

"That depends," Dave said, "on what I find at Virginia City."

They changed horses at Baker; then at Tendoy, turning up Agency Creek there. When the timber began, on more than one pine trunk Dave saw a freshly tacked poster with the words, SPOFFARD FOR SHERIFF.

At noon they lunched at Bill Sunderlin's. Before leaving Dave drew the station man aside. "Court Grady claims an alibi witness. Skinny little guy with a gold tooth; around sixty years old and ridin' a buckskin with a McClellan saddle. Ever see anyone like that pass through this canyon?"

Sunderlin shook his head. "No, and neither has anyone else. If you ask me, Grady made him up out of thin air."

This was the last station in Idaho. After a steep climb they crossed Lemhi Pass and rolled down into Montana. Light was fading when Slavin trotted his team into the Red Rock railhead.

And there Dave had luck. The train from Utah was late and hadn't arrived. By the time he'd eaten supper it came chugging in.

He boarded it and rode north to Dillon, saving time and energy. Rails were being laid on toward Butte, but just now Dillon was the end of track.

From it a six-horse stage operated easterly to Virginia City. After a night of restful sleep Dave Harbison was on it.

Most of the way it was a water grade, five hours down Beaverhead River and another five hours up Ruby Creek. Lush valleys lined the road with high piney mountains on either side. It was a range of tall grass and tumbling waters, yet Dave saw very few cattle. The men getting on and off at the change stops looked like miners.

"The pay rock's not what it usta be," the stage driver said. "You should've been here in the big rush, when Bannack and Virgie City were really turnin' out the stuff."

"If I had a chunk of this range," Dave said, "I'd stock it with cows."

"They've already done it, mister. Stock's all up in the timber now; they're savin' this valley for winter feed. Fact is they organized the Madison County Stockgrowers' Association coupla years ago and hold mixed roundups, spring and fall."

Shortly after sundown the stage left Ruby Creek and turned up Alder Gulch. Here the hillsides were scarred with shaft tailings. Another hour and the coach rattled up a dusty, slanting street between raised walks.

Virginia City! A gulch of fabulous fortunes and all his life Dave had heard about it. Clearly it had seen better days for now many of the buildings were empty. Dave saw a few ore carts, a few saddle horses, a few ranch rigs tied at the hitchracks. A sign on a store window announced the current rate of exchange for gold dust.

Beyond the store was a frame hotel with a wide, covered walk below and a railinged balcony above. As Dave's driver stopped in front of it another stagecoach rolled in from the opposite direction. "A dead heat, Sam!" one driver yelled to the other.

"It's the stage from Bozeman, in the next county east," a man told Dave.

Another night of sound sleep and he began his hunt for a man who, three years ago, had served briefly as sheriff here. The county sheriff's office was a few doors above the hotel and Dave found Edsall at his desk there. Gilroy was right. In build, coloring and bone structure this man was a physical opposite to Court Grady.

The letter Dave presented said nothing of his errand; it merely identified him as a trusted deputy of Gilroy's.

Edsall read it through. "Make yourself at home, Harbison. Anything particular on your mind?"

Dave went straight to the point. "Three years ago you were laid up with some broken ribs. Remember?"

The sheriff smiled. "How could I forget? That was a mean bronc." He held out a box of stogies. When Dave declined he lighted one himself.

"Who ran the office while you were laid up?"

"I asked my under-sheriff to take over. But he was getting married that spring and the girl wanted him to quit sheriffing. So the county commissioners appointed Bert Stanky. I never cottoned to Bert much. But no one

161

else seemed to want the job. Bert ran the office till June, when I took over again."

"Did he stay on as a deputy?"

"No. Right about that time the cowmen around here formed an association and needed an office man. The job didn't pay much but it had a high-sounding title." Edsall smiled broadly. "'Secretary-Treasurer of the Madison County Stockgrowers' Association.' Bert Stanky's the kind who likes high-sounding titles. That's why he made everybody call him sheriff while I was laid up. So Bert took the job and he's still got it. His office is up over the drugstore."

No use mentioning Court Grady, Dave decided, until he'd looked at Stanky to see if there was a facial resemblance. If there wasn't, this entire trip was a waste of time.

"Thanks, Sheriff. I'll drop in on you later."

Dave went out on the walk and saw a drugstore across the street. A second floor window had lettering on it:

MADISON COUNTY STOCKGROWERS' ASS'N
Bert Stanky: Secretary-Treas.

Since the window was open, Stanky was probably at his desk. Dave crossed to the opposite walk. Upon entering Montana he'd taken off his Idaho deputy badge. His boots and his six-gun gave him the look of a ranch hand. Stanky would take him for a rider on one of the Madison County ranches.

162

Dave entered a stairwell and went up to the second floor hall. The same lettering was on a frosted glass door at the front. The door stood slightly ajar and he went in without knocking.

The first thing he noticed was a small, steel safe. In it would be the association's funds as well as its books. Was this secretary-treasurer on the level? The man was seated at a desk, his back to Dave. Then he swiveled around and Dave saw him frontally.

Except for size he didn't seem at all like Court Grady. Grady had thick light hair. This man had no hair at all. The top of his head was like a billiard ball. No one would ever confuse him with Grady.

Dave hid his dismay and spoke merely to cover up. "You're Stanky, I take it. I'm lookin' for a ranch job. Know where I can get one?"

"The Slash C's taking on a few riders," Stanky said. "It's over on the Madison River."

"Thanks." Dave left the office and went down to the street.

He'd come to a blind end. Only Edsall or Stanky would have been addressed as sheriff here, in May of '79; the one had been in bed with broken ribs and the other simply didn't look like Grady.

Dave went back to Edsall's office for what comfort or advice he could get. But the sheriff had gone out on some errand. Dave sat down to wait, staring dismally out at the town.

Half an hour dragged by. Then Dave saw a man emerge from a stairwell across the street. A man whose face definitely reminded him of Court Grady's. Grady's chin, mouth, nose, eyes! Even the cheekbones had the contour of Grady's.

But it wasn't Grady. It was Bert Stanky!

Stanky with a hat on. And what a difference it made! The hat concealed his baldness and the shape of his upper head. It showed only the face from the eyebrows down. And that much of it was like Grady's.

Only that much of it had been seen by the Richmires. The man who'd shot and robbed Whitey Parks at a creekbank camp had been hatted — just as Stanky was now. No wonder the Richmires had called him Grady!

Upstairs, a desk table had kept Dave from seeing whether Stanky was armed. In any case he was armed now. He wore the gun like a gunman, not on the hip but on the thigh. It could be the gun which had killed Parks.

Dave saw him go into a saloon. Crossing to it, Dave looked over the half-doors and saw the man order whisky. The bartender pushed a bottle to him. "How'd yuh come out last night, Burt?"

"About fifteen bucks ahead," Stanky told him.

"That makes up fer the night before. It comes and goes, Bert."

Stanky swallowed his liquor and refilled the glass. "Yeh, first to last I guess I'm about even."

Dave went back to Edsall's office, his thoughts pumping. A night-after-night gambler, this Stanky! And the treasurer of a fund! Suppose he'd gambled away that fund a few months ago! What would he do? In a town like Virginia City he'd need to make himself

164

scarce. They'd make short shift of a trustee who embezzled a public fund.

How much was in that fund? It should be easy to find out, Dave thought. A cattlemen's association was sure to hold a meeting just before the spring roundup, which usually started late in May. At the meeting its secretary-treasurer would be called on to report.

A sign down the street told Dave where the local weekly was published. He found the editor setting type there. "When," Dave asked, "did the stockgrowers' association hold its spring meeting?"

"Eighteenth of May. Why?"

"Just want to look up the report. You printed it?"

The man grinned. "If I left it out, forty ranchers would cancel their subscriptions." He nodded toward a racked file of the current year issues. "Look at the May 22nd paper."

In ten minutes Dave went back to Edsall's office with the answer he needed. At the spring meeting, Treasurer Stanky had reported a balance on hand of $2844.50.

Suppose he'd stolen that fund and gambled it away! He'd have to run away himself before they learned of the shortage. If he'd run west to Idaho, he might get as far as Lemhi Creek by May 10th, the date of Whitey Parks' murder. Three thousand dollars worth of dust taken from Parks would be enough to cover the shortage here. Rather than become a permanent fugitive, Stanky might choose to return here and make that restitution. His entire absence from Virginia City, by horseback, need only have been seven or eight days.

165

He could have been back in time to show a proper balance at the spring meeting.

Which left just one thing to find out. When Sheriff Edsall returned from his errand Dave put it to him bluntly. "I want to know if Bert Stanky left town early in May; and if so for how long?"

Edsall didn't seem too surprised. He pursed his lips quizzically. "Does Bert need an alibi for something?"

"That's what I'm betting on. What about early in May?"

The sheriff slitted his eyes, his mind searching back. "Near as I can remember, he took a trip to Bozeman. Was gone a week or two around the middle of May."

"Who went with him?"

"Seems to me he went by himself. Said he had some private business over that way. Why?"

"My hunch is he fooled you, Sheriff, and took the opposite direction. West to Idaho. Listen." Sketchily Dave reviewed the Whitey Parks shooting and his latest ideas about it. "But if Stanky can prove he went to Bozeman, I'm wrong."

"Won't take long to check on it." Edsall got briskly to his feet. "I'll ask Sam Tanner. Sam's a stage driver between here and Bozeman. If Stanky made a saddle trip to Bozeman in May, going or coming Sam would have passed him on the trail. Sam lays over a day here between trips and he's at the hotel right now. Wait while I ask him about Stanky."

Dave waited impatiently while the sheriff went to the hotel. Across the street he saw Stanky come out of the saloon and go back to his office.

166

Then Edsall reappeared, looking grimly convinced. "Sam can't remember passing Stanky on the Bozeman road any time this year. But that's not all. At the hotel I ran into Nelson Story."

"Who's he?"

"He's the biggest cattleman in Gallatin County. Lives at Bozeman. Right now he's over here trying to lease some Madison County grass. I asked him if he saw Bert Stanky on the streets of Bozeman in May. He said no."

"So Stanky lied about going there!"

"Probably. But we haven't proved it yet. He could've been in Bozeman without either Sam or Nelse Story seeing him. The proof's up to Stanky himself. Let's go pin him down."

They went up to Stanky's office and found him at his desk. The man was hatless now, and again Dave had a sense of dismay. The shiny dome made him look so little like Court Grady.

Edsall wasted no time. "Where were you on the tenth of May, Bert?"

"Bozeman." The answer was prompt and confident. Dave watched the man's eyes for some sign of panic; but there seemed to be only a mild puzzlement.

"Can you name three people," Edsall asked bluntly, "who saw you in Bozeman between the fifth and fifteenth of May?"

"What's the matter, Sheriff? Did someone steal a horse about that time? Who saw me in Bozeman? Plenty of people. Let's see: I put my horse up at Ed Fridley's livery barn. Ed'll have a record of it. Ran into

Sheriff McKinzie a couple of times. He asked about *you*, Sheriff. Stopped at the Laclede Hotel and had a drink at the bar there with Postmaster Taylor; he asked how the mail service was over this way. And oh yes, I bought a pair of spurs at Charlie Rich's store and paid for 'em with a check. Oughta be right here, somewhere." Stanky opened a drawer and began sifting through a batch of cancelled checks.

To Dave it seemed a little too glib. The man had rattled off the names of four top citizens at Bozeman, not to mention the staff and guests of the leading hotel.

"Here it is, Sheriff." Stanky produced a cancelled check for seven dollars. It was dated May tenth, the very date of Park's murder. The check was endorsed by the Rich Mercantile Company of Bozeman and had cleared through the Bozeman bank a day later.

Edsall examined it, handed it back with a cryptic smile. "Looks like I made a mistake, Bert. Sorry I bothered you."

With Dave he went back to his office and there he fairly crackled with suspicions. "He reeled off those, names too fast! As for the check, he could've bought those spurs by mail. I mean if he planned a runaway west, he could mail a small check to a town east of here. When it cleared it would pull us in a wrong direction."

"You'll ask at Bozeman?"

"You bet. First I'll hustle up the street and put the whole thing before the county attorney. We'll write letters to Fridley, Taylor, McKinzie and Rich, and get 'em off by special courier. You stay here and keep an eye on Stanky's office. I don't think he'll run for it. But if he tries to, stop him."

Edsall hurried up the street to confer with other county officers. Dave, waiting for him to come back, took his post on the front walk to watch windows over the drugstore.

The angle kept him from seeing Stanky at his desk. And presently he began wondering if the man was still there. Maybe he'd left by way of back stairs. He'd have good reason to, if he'd faked those Bozeman alibis.

To make sure, Dave crossed the street and went up steps to a hallway. The door to Stanky's office was closed. When he tried the knob, Dave found it locked.

What was Stanky doing in there behind a locked door? Or was he there at all? Dave rapped on the frosted glass and got no answer. Then he drew his gun and smashed out a segment of glass with the barrel.

A look through the jagged hole told Dave the office was empty. So Stanky had slipped away by an alley exit! He could be out of the county by the time a courier made a round trip to Bozeman.

Then Dave saw the clincher. Stanky hadn't gone away empty-handed. For the door of a small steel safe now stood ajar! An hour ago it was locked. So Stanky had taken with him whatever fund had been kept there.

Dave raced down the hall and found steps to an alley. A wagon stood at the drugstore's rear door. Its teamster was unloading merchandise and Dave asked him breathlessly, "Where does Bert Stanky keep his horse?"

"Cooper's livery barn." The teamster pointed east up the alley.

Dave ran that way till he came to the back door of a public stable. Looking in he saw Stanky. The man had just led a horse from its stall and was throwing on a saddle. This time he wore a leather camp jacket and there was a travel roll tied back of the cantle.

"Off for Bozeman again, Stanky?"

Dave's challenge made the man spin toward him, hand swinging toward the grip of a low-holstered gun.

"I wouldn't try it," Dave warned. "Better not try a run-out, either. Because I've got orders."

"Orders from who?"

"From the sheriff. He said if you try a run-out, I'm to stop you. Why don't we just both wait here, calm and peaceable, till he gets back and takes over?"

Stanky's hand slapped at the butt of his gun, got it clear of the holster as Dave fired his own. There was only the one shot, followed by a bellow of pain as Bert Stanky went down with a bullet-smashed arm.

CHAPTER
SEVENTEEN

"He had a wad of money on him, Lisa. The stockgrowers' fund they'd kept in the safe; close to three thousand dollars."

It was three days after the gunfight with Stanky and Dave had just arrived on Jake Slavin's stage. Lisa, Laura and Sheriff Gilroy were in the hotel parlor with him, listening to his report.

"It proves Dad didn't do it!" Lisa cried joyfully.

"To me it does," Dave assured her. "What about you, Sheriff?"

"It's not me that counts," Gilroy said. "It's Judge Corry. He's the one who passed sentence. If the Richmires look Stanky in the face, with his hat on, and say be *might* be the man they saw shoot Whitey Parks, I think Corry'll call it a mistrial. Any retrial oughta clear Grady."

"Then why," Lisa asked Dave, "didn't you bring Stanky back with you for the Richmires to look at?"

"I wanted to," Dave said, "but Edsall turned me down. He says Montana has a solid larceny case against Stanky and they're holding him for it. Idaho has no case against him at all unless we issue a murder warrant; which we can't do until the Richmires identify him. Even then we'd have to extradite him, governor to governor."

"He's right," Gilroy said. "Tell you what I'll do, Lisa. I'll get a private conveyance and drive the Richmires to Virginia City. Maybe I can get Judge Corry to go along; either him or the county attorney."

"Can't you hurry?" Lisa begged. "How long will it take?"

"Five to seven days for the round trip," Gilroy reckoned. "If we go part of the way by train, and make good connections like Dave did, we can beat that a little."

By the tension on Lisa's face Dave knew she was measuring time — the short time left them on a thirty-day reprieve. A scaffold tower still stood in the jailyard.

To comfort her Dave brought a paper from his pocket. "On the way home, while waiting for a train at Dillon, I made a full report of what I ran into at Virginia City. Made two copies. One for you, Sheriff." He passed the paper to Gilroy. "Mailed the other one to Governor Neil at Boise."

Laura Kane slipped an arm around Lisa and the girl relaxed a little. "I hope you emphasized the resemblance," Laura said, "between Stanky and Court Grady."

"I bore down on it," Dave assured them.

"I better go see Judge Corry right now," Gilroy said. "And the county attorney. And let's not tell anyone about this until I say so."

He hurried out.

172

Dave made a cigarette and the two women could see that something bothered him. "If we're right," he said, "it wraps up the Whitey Parks' case — except for one angle!"

"What?" Laura asked him.

"Stanky couldn't've had anything to do with the shooting of my brother; nor with the rash of placer raids over around Leesburg. And yet we thought all three of those things were linked, somehow."

"But there's no link to Stanky!" Laura agreed.

"Which means we're still missing a bet," Dave worried. "Know where Buck Blanchard is?"

They didn't, and presently Dave went looking for him. He found the big deputy nursing a schooner of beer at Pope's bar.

After briefing Blanchard about Bert Stanky, Dave asked, "What happened while I was gone, Buck?"

"This." Blanchard produced a letter which was postmarked Hailey. "Gilroy didn't tell you about it just now at the hotel, because he didn't want to bring it up in front of Laura Kane."

As he read the letter a slow anger flushed Dave. It was an answer to one he'd written the *LD* ranch, asking when and to whom they'd sold a certain sorrel horse.

A man walked into the ranchyard lugging his saddle. It was late in April two years ago. He said his mount had foundered up the trail a piece and he wanted to buy another. Gave his name as J. V. Brown. We sold him the sorrel and gave him a

173

bill-of-sale. Our memory is that he was a tall dark man between thirty and forty years old.

"He was Marv Kane!" The last doubt of it left Dave. No wonder Gilroy had avoided mention of it before Laura! She'd broken with him long ago; but it would still hurt her to learn he'd murdered Gregg Harbison.

The letter definitely put Kane in the Hailey area at the time of Gregg's death. It proved he'd ridden the two hundred miles to Hailey so hard and fast that he'd foundered his horse; and that he'd lied about buying the sorrel from an immigrant on the Blackfoot road.

It made a pattern with everything Dave had learned from Packy Blue and Ed Bellamy. How could anyone doubt, now, that Kane had suspected his wife of running away to join Gregg at his distant placer claim, and had ridden there on a fast, furious mission of revenge?

Except for one small thing Dave would have been stonily sure of it. A missing link. The same vague, illusive thread which failed to tie the known guilt of Bert Stanky to two other guilts.

"What's Gilroy going to do about it, Buck?"

"Gilroy always liked Marv Kane," Buck said. "This looks like the deadwood, all right, but he thinks Marv oughta have a chance to explain. So this afternoon he sent word to the Kaybar asking Kane to come in. Didn't say why; just said he wanted to ask a few questions."

At the far end of the bar two men were dicing for the drinks. Sight of one of them recalled a dimly puzzling

174

detail to Dave. "That's Mitchell, the assayer, isn't it? Who's the man with him?"

"A lawyer named Lillard," Buck said.

Lillard! Dave remembered where he'd heard the name before. "Look, Buck. What's up at the head of Geerston Creek, besides grizzly bears?"

Blanchard stared vacantly and Dave had to repeat the question. "A five-man bear hunt was set for that place, the day after I hit town. They postponed it a month."

"What's wrong with that?"

"Chuck Spoffard and four town men," Dave said. "Spoffard set it up and is furnishing the pack stock. Ever been up there, Buck?"

"To the head of Geerston? Once — and I hope I never go again. It's a horse-killing trail with some mean rock slides and ledges. Had to lead my bronc across those slides; and by the time I got home I had bunions."

"No one lives up there?"

"Not since old man Shumaker gave up and went back east. That was seven or eight years ago. He had a puny little quartz vein up there but it played out on him. It's way up at the top of that canyon, dang near to the Bitterroot divide."

"Did he have a cabin?"

"A sod-roof shack, as I remember. What's it got to do with grizzly bears?"

"I don't know, Buck. Let me chew on it a while. Anything else happen while I was gone?"

"Not here. But they had a break up at Leesburg. Remember that posse I took off with? We split; I followed one man and the rest of them followed three. They caught up with 'em at Yellowjacket Creek and had a gunfight."

"How did it come out?"

"Two of 'em got away; disappeared into the wilderness area beyond Middle Fork. Other one stopped a bullet and they picked him up dead. They identified him as a long-wanted killer from Oregon named Trego."

Dave barely heard. He was watching Mitchell and Lillard. Each man paid for a round of drinks and each was offered a choice of two cards. Each dropped his chosen card into a box of straw ballots.

"When are you going to count 'em?" Lillard asked.

"Next Saturday night," the bartender said.

As the two went out Dave turned thoughtfully to Blanchard. "Let's you and I take a ride, Buck."

"To Yellowjacket?"

"No. Opposite direction. To the top of Geerston Creek."

"That's a helluva trail," Buck demurred. "Take us from sunup till dark."

"And another day to get back," Dave agreed. "But maybe we'll find something up there."

"Such as what?"

"Such as the reason Chuck Spoffard put off a bear hunt."

When Dave explained what he meant, Buck stared blankly for a moment. "It's a long shot, pardner. With

176

us gone, and Gilroy off to Montana, there won't be anybody to mind the office 'cept the jailer."

"Which won't hurt him any," Dave argued, "because right now he's only got one prisoner; and Court Grady never gives him any trouble."

"Okay," Blanchard agreed grumpily. "I'll have two stout horses ready at sunup; and some grub packs. Like I said, it's all ledges and rock slides up there. Time we get back we'll have bunions."

CHAPTER
EIGHTEEN

A special dawn breakfast for five men was served at the hotel. An air of mystery surrounded it and even the waitress failed to catch a word of the guarded talk.

The five went out to a double-seated buckboard and two saddled horses. For a few minutes they stood in low, earnest discussion; then one of them, Judge Aaron Corry, left the others and walked home.

Sheriff Gilroy and County Attorney Copeland climbed on the buckboard and drove out of town, taking the upvalley stage road toward Tendoy. The other two, Deputies Blanchard and Harbison, followed on horseback.

The departure started a buzz of rumors. Apparently some new and important development was on tap.

"Judge Corry himself saw 'em off! Wonder where to!"

"Must have somethin' to do with that trip young Harbison took to Montana."

"I hear the sheriff got a letter from Hailey, the other day. A new lead on an old killing down there, I heard. Might be they're headin' for Hailey to check on it."

Actually only the buckboard went more than eight miles up the stage road. There, at the crossing of

Geerston Creek, the two horsemen stopped and let the buckboard continue on upvalley toward the Richmire homestead.

Dave rolled a smoke while his mount drooped its head to drink. "Take a good look at the country close by here, Buck. Suppose you're an old man hiding out in a cabin at the head of Geerston Gulch. You run out of grub so you ride down to the valley to get some. You don't dare let anyone see you, so your only chance is to steal some at a ranch where nobody's at home. Maybe a ham, a sack of flour or beans. You get this far — and what do you see?"

"I see the Mulkey ranch a mile downvalley; and the Grady place a mile upvalley."

"A big ranch and a little one, Buck. Lots of folks at the big ranch but only one man at the little one. If he's not at home you can prowl there without being seen. But he *is* at home and he sees you; so you cover up by pretending to be lost. You ask how far is it to Haystack Mountain? or any place else just so it's a long way from Geerston Creek. Then you beat it back to your hideout. And the reason no one sees you on the stage road is because you only used the mile of it between here and Grady's gate."

They rode up Geerston and for the first few miles the trail was fairly smooth. Then they struck timber at the toe of the Bitterroot Range. Soon they were in a narrow, rocky gulch.

Buck, in the lead, twisted in his saddle to look back. "You're playin' a long shot, pardner. Old man

Shumaker quit that shack eight years ago. He went east and nobody's seen him since."

"Eight years," Dave countered, "is long enough for a man to get in trouble. If he needs a hideout, and his name's Shumaker, he knows right where to hide. A little man with a gold tooth, Grady said."

"He was a little guy," Buck admitted. "But I don't recollect any gold tooth."

"Maybe he didn't have one eight years ago."

The gulch narrowed and made them cross back and forth from one side of the creek to the other. Steep piney slopes pinched in on them. More than once a sheer wall forced them to leave the stream and detour along a ledge far upslope. "You asked for it, pardner," Buck grinned. "It gets worse, further up."

Noon found them resting at a waterfall. The horses stood by, heads down and jaded. Cascades above and below made Dave raise his voice. "Is this a good bear country, Buck?"

"As good as any," the big man shouted back.

They trailed on; and at the top of the next cascade a rock slide forced them to dismount.

With Blanchard picking up the way they led the horses step by precarious step across it, loose rock sliding under their feet, and came at last to a glen beyond. Here the creek was less noisy and Dave could speak without shouting.

"Ever strike you as funny, Buck, that Spoffard would rig up a bear hunt right in the middle of an election campaign?"

180

"Take him at least a week," Buck admitted, "gettin' that party up here, baggin' a couple of grizzlies, skinnin' 'em and then trailin' back to town."

"He rigged it up *twice!* Each time right after a hanging date!"

Above the glen they came to another rock slide. Again Buck dismounted to lead his horse. "It's shank's mare from here on, fella."

"No wonder they don't run cattle up here!" Dave said.

Lodgepole pine was so dense they could barely see the sky. On and up they trailed, afoot and leading the horses, often over treacherous slides. Light began fading and the air cooled, meaning it was past sundown. Twice Dave saw bear sign and once he glimpsed a band of mountain sheep.

In the next glen the creek split. "They call the right fork Cary Creek," Buck said. "We take the left."

The skyline of the Bitterroot divide loomed close, dead ahead of them. But along this left fork they found the going a little easier, with spots of grass and an occasional copse of aspen.

There was an hour of twilight left when they turned a bend and came into a small mountain park. Beaver had made a series of aspen-bough dams and near these pools the blue-stem grew knee high.

But it had been grazed, Dave saw. From an aspen clump ahead came the whinny of a horse.

In a minute they sighted it — a buckskin with the forelegs hobbled. The animal was in fair flesh. But it had a frightened look. Its whinny seemed strangely plaintive and even frantic as it came hobbling toward the two saddled mounts.

Buck looked at bruises on the forelegs. "Them hobbles 've been on a long time," he concluded.

A hundred yards farther on they came to a small shack with rock walls and a sod roof. Its door was shut and it looked deserted.

"Shumaker's?" Dave asked as they approached.

Buck nodded. He dismounted and pushed the door open. Out of it came the stench of unattended death.

In the dimness of the one room the first thing Dave saw was an old army saddle. A McClellan.

The room had a dirt floor. There was a homemade bunk, a rude chair and table, all made of aspen boughs. The table had a kerosene lantern and Blanchard lighted it.

A man on the bunk had been a long time dead. He lay face up under blankets in a position of repose, with no sign of violence on or about him. On a table within reach of the bunk were a water bucket and some medicine bottles. Apparently the man died of some natural sickness, alone here.

The one conclusive thing about him was a prominent gold tooth.

A wallet on the table had a little money. So no robbery was involved.

"Mountain fever, maybe," Buck muttered. "He expected to get well or he wouldn't've left them hobbles on his horse. Better go take 'em off, Dave. Then you can unsaddle and make camp while I look him over."

Dave was glad enough to get out into fresh air. He caught the buckskin, unhobbled it. The grateful animal shook its hide, neighed, then rolled in the grass there.

Dave chose a campsite a hundred yards from the shack. After picketing the horses he made a fire and unrolled the grub packs. Dusk was closing in when Blanchard came toward him with a lighted lantern.

"I'd say he's been dead more'n a month," Buck reported. "Maybe two. Not a mark on him and the shack hasn't been raided. He's Shumaker all right. Look."

He handed Dave a scrap of paper he'd found in a coat hanging on the cabin wall. It was a receipted bill for a purchase made by Court Grady at the Shoup store in Salmon City. On the back of it was a rude pencil sketch showing the way from Grady's ranch on Lemhi Creek to Haystack Mountain, at the head of Camp Creek beyond Leesburg.

"Fits like the paper on the wall," Buck said. "Blows the case against Grady sky high. We've hit pay rock, pardner."

"It's a *bonanza!*" Dave exulted; and he wasn't thinking of a sketch or a gold tooth. A human life was worth more than gold and beyond any doubt they'd saved Grady's. For here was the man's alibi witness. With the Stanky resemblance to support it, Grady's release should be only a matter of routine.

Blanchard put a can of water on the fire. "But I still don't savvy the bear hunt," he puzzled.

Dave waited till bacon was sizzling. "The bear hunt," he reminded Buck, "was set for the day after Grady's

183

hanging. The hunters would find Shumaker's body here and then the whole county would know the hanging was a mistake. I figure Spoffard wanted it that way. He dated the bear hunt to make it happen like that. When the hangin' was put off a month, he put off the bear hunt the same month. The postponed hunt would turn up the same proof — a day too late!"

Buck was still puzzled. "But how could Spoffard know about the old man bein' up here dead?"

"Maybe he was curious and came up here for a look. He could put two and two together, just like I did. If a man on a buckskin horse came down from some Bitterroot hideaway, Geerston was the most likely gulch to bring him out near Grady's place." Another possibility struck Dave and his wits tangled with it a moment. "Or maybe," he suggested, "somebody working for Spoffard, like a wolf hunter named Budlong, found a dead man up here and told Spoffard about it. Don't forget it was Budlong who helped Brushy-Chin hold up that stage."

"This is wolf country," Buck admitted. "But what the Sam Hill would Spoffard gain by it?"

"He's running for sheriff against Gilroy. If Gilroy hangs Grady, and the next day it turns out to be a mistake, how would people feel about it?"

"They'd blame Gilroy," Buck admitted, "for botchin' the case and hangin' the wrong man. So they'd vote for Spoffard by a landslide."

It might even be unanimous, they agreed after talking it over. For Ad Gilroy was deeply sensitive. In remorse and humiliation, he might in such a case

184

withdraw from the race and let Spoffard run unopposed.

"Chuck'll swear he didn't know the old man was up here," Buck said. "And we can never prove he did."

"All we got on him is a motive," Dave agreed. And motives weren't always conclusive. Tony Sebastian had a solid money motive for sending agents to hold up a stage and delay a reprieve.

"We'll have a talk with Chuck when we get to town," Buck decided. "Likely we'll find Marv Kane there too, waitin' to see Gilroy."

Kane had been sent for, Dave remembered, to be questioned about a trip to Hailey two years ago. Which pulled Dave's mind away from the Whitey Parks' case and pinned it again on Gregg Harbison's. Pinky Ogle had touched off a link between those two crimes. Apparently Bert Stanky had killed Parks for money, Kane had killed Gregg for revenge, and Spoffard had conspired to cheat justice. Delaying a reprieve and rigging up a bear hunt to uncover evidence a day too late — these were treacheries of the same stripe. But there was still a missing key, Dave thought. It would need some bigger prize than a sheriff's badge to make Spoffard take all that trouble and risk.

They spread blankets by the fire and turned in for the night. Gilroy and Copeland, Dave hoped, by now were riding a train with the Richmires from Red Rock to Dillon. From there a second private conveyance would take them on to Virginia City. Would the Richmires identify Stanky? It would help if they merely

185

admitted a doubt. In any case there'd still be a gold-toothed dead man to witness for Court Grady.

Off down the Bitterroot divide a panther screamed. Three picketed horses champed restlessly. Panthers, wolves and grizzly bears! No wonder the hobbled buckskin had welcomed company! For more than a month up here it had been at the mercy of flesh-eating beasts. Hobbled, it could hardly have made its way past those rock slides and downcanyon to the valley.

"There's a tarp in the shack," Buck said drowsily. "Tomorrow we'll wrap up the old man and pack him out on his own horse."

CHAPTER
NINETEEN

Dave used half the morning searching for sign around the glen. He wanted proof that Spoffard or an agent of Spoffard's had been here. All he found was the ashes of a campfire. It was a one-man camp made earlier this season; but nothing had been dropped to identify the camper. While Dave searched; Buck Blanchard packed the buckskin with the tarp-wrapped remains of its master.

The rock slides and ledges, with an extra horse to coax along them, made slow going. It was dark when they hit the stage road near the Mulkey ranch. The Mulkey crew gave them supper and the deputies pushed on, trailing into town near midnight.

Blanchard pulled up at the cottage of Doctor Flint, county coroner. It was unlighted. "I'll have to wake him up, Dave, and ask what he wants done with the body. You better shag on and tell Lisa."

"Thanks, Buck." Dave hurried on to the hotel.

Lisa, the clerk told him, had gone to bed. "She and Mrs. Kane both. They drove a buggy out to the Grady ranch today and tidied the place up. New window curtains and clean sheets on the bed." The clerk grinned. "That's just how sure they are he'll be goin' home pretty soon."

187

"They'll be still surer," Dave said, "after they hear from me."

He took the steps three at a time and knocked on Lisa's door.

At his second knock she answered sleepily. "Who is it?"

"It's Dave. Wake up and celebrate, Lisa. I got good news."

She supposed he meant good news from Virginia City. When she'd dressed and let him in, Dave told her about Geerston Gulch. "Which double-cinches it, Lisa!"

"Does Dad know?" she asked breathlessly.

"No. I just got in."

"Please let's go tell him now."

The girl threw on a cloak and they went down to the street. Hand in hand they hurried through its dust to the jail. The street door was locked and they had to bang on it.

When the jailer let them in grumpily, Lisa rushed by him and back to her father's cell. The jailer started to follow but Dave stopped him. "Let *her* tell him, Pop. She'll want to cry a little; and maybe he will too."

Pop Sweeney had brought a shotgun to the door and Dave eyed it with a smile. "Who did you think we were, Pop? A lynch party?"

"Nope," Sweeney said. "But I been kinda leery since what happened at suppertime yesterday."

"What was that?"

"I was feedin' Grady when I heard a shot up the alley. Took a look but couldn't find anyone out there.

188

But when I got back I found a sneak caller had slipped in at the front."

"Yeh? Who was he?"

The jailer shrugged. "How would *I* know? All he did was open that storage closet and frisk an outfit of clothes in there. Pinky Ogle's duds. Turned the pockets inside out and ripped the linings."

"Makes three times," Dave brooded. Someone was still after the "proof" mentioned by Ogle during the last minute of his life. Proof bearing on the murder of Gregg Harbison! A search at Ogle's shanty; a search at Ogle's bar; now a search of the man's garments at the jail.

"Lock up that closet, Pop, and hide the key."

Dave went back to where Lisa was talking through bars to her father. "We began fixing up your house today, Dad; Laura and I." The girl turned eagerly to Dave. "They'll be letting him out right away, won't they?"

"I'm no lawyer," Dave said. "I guess they'll wait till Gilroy and Copeland get back from Montana. Then they'll go into a huddle with Judge Corry. Likely the judge won't waste much time after that. He was the one who passed sentence. He'll know it was a mistake and he won't sleep very well till he corrects it. I'd better go see him right now and tell him about that witness."

"*Your* witness, Dad!" Lisa exulted. "The one they said you made up."

"He must've died in bed soon after you saw him, Mr. Grady," Dave said. "It's the same man, all right, gold tooth and all."

"Makes three times," the prisoner murmured gratefully, unaware that he echoed words just spoken by Dave to the jailer. "Three times you saved my life." His hand reached through the bars and gripped Dave's.

Lisa was impatient. "Please hurry, Dave, and go tell Judge Corry."

She kissed her father goodnight and they went out through the front office. In passing Dave spoke again to Pop Sweeney. "Did Marvin Kane come to town? Gilroy sent for him."

"Haven't seen him," the jailer said.

"Don't forget to lock up that closet."

Again Dave and Lisa walked hand in hand up the street. "What's in the closet?" she asked.

"The duds Pinky Ogle had on. Pinky claimed he had some secret proof and it's got somebody on pins and needles."

"Why did the sheriff send for Mr. Kane?"

"Wants to ask him a few questions." Dave clipped his answer short and made no mention of a letter from the *LD* ranch; a letter which seemed to incriminate Marvin Kane. If Lisa knew she might tell Laura. Until the full story was in there was no use in disturbing Laura with it.

"What made you go up Geerston Creek, Dave?"

And again Dave told her less than the full story. He said nothing about his unproven theory that Chuck Spoffard had twice scheduled a bear hunt to expose proof of innocence — not before, but *after*, the hanging of Court Grady. Tonight of all nights, a thing so

190

inhumanly brutal as that shouldn't be inflicted upon a young and sensitive girl.

He parted from her at the hotel and went on to Judge Corry's house. Routed out of bed the judge listened gravely to Dave's story. "Blanchard was with me," Dave finished. "He took the body to the coroner."

Corry used his sleeve to mop sweat beads from his brow. His voice was shaky but cautiously noncommittal. "Thanks, young man. I'll discuss it with the county attorney when he gets back. Perhaps he, too, will have new evidence. Goodnight."

Back at the hotel Dave found Buck Blanchard at the bar. The big man beckoned. "Join me in a nightcap, Dave, while we figure out what we'd better say to that bear hunter."

It was a delicate question and they huddled half an hour over it. They could hardly accuse Spoffard. Dave's idea about the bear hunt was only a guess. If it was a wrong guess they'd look stupid. If it was a right guess they'd be warning Spoffard prematurely, with nothing solid to charge him with.

"So we'd better sleep on it," Buck decided.

They slept late and it was midmorning when they rode up the Salmon River. "The Box Q's only six or seven miles," Buck said. "Right above where Williams Creek comes in."

"Isn't that near where you lost those tracks, last week? The raider you trailed over the pass from the placer country?"

"That's right. He rode into the river near Spoffard's place. But he couldn't be one of Spoffard's crew."

"Why not?"

"He was riding a mule. Cowboys don't ride mules."

"How big's the Box Q?"

"Around seven hundred head. Top grade stuff. Only two regular hands between roundups. For the spring and fall gathers Chuck picks up a few more."

They'd decided on three questions to ask Spoffard. Could he come into town and look at a dead man found up Geerston Creek? The coroner wanted an identification. Had Frank Budlong been up this way lately? A report was that he'd been seen fording the Salmon River on a mule. And from his memory of the Kaybar ranch two years ago, could he say when and why Marvin Kane had made a fast round-trip ride to Hailey?

"He'll answer 'Why are you asking me?'" Dave predicted.

"If he does," Buck decided, "we'll let on like it's the coroner wants to know, not us."

To one or more of the questions Spoffard might react guiltily, Dave hoped. A slip could give him away.

They came to the Box Q gate, passed through it and crossed a pasture. The building layout stood well back from the river, nestling between foothills. There was a rock dwelling, solid and square, with a ditch running by it. It made one side of a quadrangle with a pulley well at the center. A stable and bunkhouse made another side; a row of feed sheds made another side with a corral on the fourth.

There wasn't a man in sight. The corral had only one horse and Buck recognized it as a livery mount from Kingsbury's stable in town. "Somebody's out here visitin', pardner."

They tied their mounts and tapped at the house door. The man who opened it had a cigar in his mouth and didn't belong here.

Buck blinked his surprise. "Hi! Who-all's at home?"

The man grinned. "Nobody but me and the cook. Come on in."

He was the paunchy cattle buyer, Whipple, who'd ridden out of Red Rock on a stage with Dave. They joined him in the ranch parlor where the man ensconced himself in a rocker. Fresh cigar butts indicated that he'd been making himself at home for quite a while.

"Whatcha doin' out here?" Buck asked him.

"Buyin' cattle." Whipple puffed smoke into rings.

"From Chuck Spoffard?"

"That's right. He and his crew are up the valley bunchin' 'em right now."

"How many are you buying?"

"All of 'em." Whipple had a smug look, Dave thought. "The shebang. The whole Box Q brand, horn and hoof."

Blanchard eyed him narrowly. "You came up on your bid, huh? Last I heard you were ten dollars under the market."

The man chuckled. "I never raised it a nickel. Spoffard looked me up in town yesterday and said okay; if I'd show up this morning he'd tally 'em out to me, every hoof, at my own price."

The deputies exchanged alert glances. Had something warned Spoffard? Why was he in such a hurry to sell out?

When they asked, Whipple had a ready answer. "It's none of my business why." With a pleased look he brought out cigars and offered them. Buck took one and Dave waved them aside. "It's the way I operate," the buyer grinned, "and generally it pays off."

"Pays off how?" Dave prompted.

"I go to a range and bid for cattle at a dozen ranches. Always bid plenty below the market. Then I sit back and wait."

"Wait for what?"

"For the law of averages to start workin'. Out of a dozen cowmen, there'll always be one with a reason for raising cash quick. Maybe to pay off a debt; maybe on account of his health; maybe he's in trouble over some woman. What for is none of my business. This time I thought it would be Kane of the Kaybar; but it turned out to be Spoffard."

Again the deputies exchanged glances. Spoffard, it seemed, had the wind up. Did he think they knew more than they really did?

"When do you look for him back?" Buck asked.

"Middle of the afternoon, maybe. The stuff was mostly bunched yesterday and it's only a few miles upvalley."

"Dave and I want to see him too," Buck said. "So we might as well hang around." He picked up a magazine and sat down with it.

194

A slight uneasiness pricked Dave. "How many men rode out with Spoffard?"

"Just the two regular hands," Whipple said.

Spoffard himself made three — enough to bring the cattle in for a tally. Yet the uneasiness persisted. "Since we've got to wait we'd better unsaddle." Dave beckoned Blanchard to join him outside.

The big deputy followed him to the hitchrack. "Do you know 'em, Buck?"

Buck nodded. He took the saddle from his horse and draped it over the hitchrail. "Chet Lucas and a guy they call Limpy. Run-of-the-mill cowhands."

"Have they ever been in trouble?"

"None I ever heard of."

"If we have to arrest Spoffard, would they back him in a gunplay?"

Blanchard gave it thought as he rolled a cigarette. "My guess is they wouldn't; not for forty dollars a month."

Dave took a rifle from each of the saddle scabbards. "Just to play safe, let's hang on to our hardware."

They went back into the house where Whipple looked curiously as Dave set two rifles in a corner. "It's blowing up for a rain," Dave explained, "and we don't want 'em to rust."

"I make dinner for you, *signors*. How do you like the steak?"

It was the Bar Q cook who appeared in an inner doorway with a cup towel wrapped around his middle. He was a thin little man with a curved black mustache. An Italian, Dave guessed.

"Make mine rare," the cattle buyer said.

"Well done for me," Buck said, and Dave echoed him.

The cook went back to the kitchen. "Name's Guiseppe," Buck told Dave. "Used to work at the International Hotel."

Dave wondered why he'd quit. A hotel would pay more than a ranch.

Whipple went to a window and looked out. "Can't see any rain clouds," he said. Dave ignored him. This pot-bellied beef buyer didn't count one way or another.

Buck asked curiously, "Is this a cash deal?"

"Spot cash." Whipple turned from the window with a grin. "You can always make a cheaper buy that way."

"You've got it with you?"

"I've got a checkbook with me. And the money's in the Salmon City bank. Spoffard made sure of it before he closed the deal."

Again the deputies exchanged glances. More and more it looked like the cash-in for a fast getaway.

Whipple was still at the window. "Someone's comin' through the gate," he announced. "Looks like Marvin Kane."

Dave looked out and saw it was true. A single rider cantered toward the house. He was Kane of the Kaybar riding an *LD* sorrel; a mount he'd bought two years ago near Hailey, after a hard, secret ride there.

Kane tied his horse at the front rack. Dave opened the door for him. The rancher came in, showing no surprise when he found two deputies there. "Hello, Buck. Gilroy sent for me but when I got to town he was

196

gone. So I asked for you and Sweeney said you rode out to the Box Q. What did Ad want to see me about?"

To Dave he didn't look at all like a shoot-from-the-bush killer.

Blanchard gave a blunt answer. "*This*." He handed Kane the letter from the *LD* ranch. "Sit down and read it."

Kane read it standing. He was armed with a holster gun and Dave kept a sharp watch. "Maybe you can explain," Buck said grimly.

A trapped look came into Kane's eyes. He handed the letter back and sat down. When he answered his tone was bleak. "I might've known you'd find out some day."

Then he turned with a desperate appeal to Dave. "You're his brother. I know what you think. But you're wrong. I didn't do it. Honest to God I didn't."

"You're a little late," Dave challenged. "You waited till we caught you in a lie."

"I was a fool!" Kane said bitterly. "A stupid, drunken fool! And it might've been even worse. I might have killed Gregg Harbison. But I didn't!"

"Wasn't that what you went down there for?" Dave demanded.

Kane didn't deny it. "Only if I found Laura with him! But she wasn't. When I searched his cabin I knew she'd never been there. There wasn't even a letter from her. I knew I'd been wrong about it all along."

"So you hit for home?"

"So fast I killed my horse and had to get another one. And so ashamed I didn't dare tell where I'd been."

Buck fixed a shrewd gaze on him. "Did you see Gregg Harbison down there?"

"No. His cabin was empty. I was back home at the Kaybar when news came he'd been shot. Maybe it was before I called there, maybe it was after."

"Why should I believe you?" Dave asked him.

"You can believe what you want." Kane looked pleadingly from Dave to Blanchard. "But please don't tell Laura — yet. She's got reason enough to hate me — but she doesn't know I made that ride to Hailey."

"She'll *have* to know, some time," Buck said. "The killing was in another county and we'll have to send them the facts. When we do, the Hailey sheriff'll show up with a warrant."

"Give me that long, anyway," Kane begged. "Just don't tell Laura till you have to."

"We've got one other suspect," Dave told him.

The Kaybar man looked up eagerly. "Who?"

"A man who made a trip to Denver about that time. And who came back with enough money to buy this ranch. A man who held up a reprieve and then postponed a bear hunt!" Dave looked at Whipple who sat by, eyes bugging. "And now he's making a fast sellout. When he shows up we'll ask him why."

A burst of alarmed questions came from Whipple. "You mean he's not on the level? He bought his outfit with crooked money? Then to hell with him! The deal's off. I won't get mixed up with . . ."

"Shut up!" Dave glanced toward the kitchen where a cook might have sharp ears. He lowered his own voice.

198

"Stay out of this, Whipple. And Kane, we won't tell Laura till we have to — on one condition."

"Name it," Kane said.

"It's this: if we turn up something on Spoffard and he gets tough, you'll help Buck and me handle him."

"He's got two men," Blanchard put in. "Maybe more. On a showdown Dave and I'd be outnumbered."

"I'll side you," Kane promised.

"Dinner she is ready, *signors*. I have set another plate." Guiseppe stood in the dining room doorway, a moist smile on his face.

"Let's eat," Buck said heartily.

They went in to a table set for four. Guiseppe served them steak and fried potatoes. After they'd eaten a while he came in with a pot of strong coffee and filled the cups.

The drowsiness came over Dave about five minutes later. Blanchard, he noticed, had a dopey look. So did Whipple and Kane. Kane's mouth hung open and his chin sagged on his chest. Beyond him Dave saw a sly, Italian face peer in from the kitchen.

He tried to stand up but his muscles wouldn't react. A creeping paralysis came over him and he knew why — too late. He saw Blanchard's huge frame slither sideways. After that he knew nothing at all.

CHAPTER
TWENTY

A long time went by and then Dave felt a damp touch on his face. Someone was rubbing a rag over it. Dimly he heard voices — voices which weren't Buck's or Kane's or Whipple's. He saw Blanchard on his feet, groping with his legs wide apart, his eyes staring stupidly at someone. Whipple sat with his head bowed forward on his arms. The man on the floor was Kane.

"What on earth happened?" The voice was like Lisa Grady's! But it couldn't be! What would Lisa be doing out here?

A soft hand touched Dave's cheek and a glass of water was held to his lips. "Who did it, Dave?" It was Lisa bending over him.

He was sitting on the dining room floor with his back to a wall. A table set for four helped him to remember.

"Where did he go, Lisa? The cook?"

"No one's here but us," she said. "We drove up in a buggy just now."

Slowly Dave's wits began to gather. The cook must have doped them and gone off to warn Spoffard. He saw Laura Kane kneeling beside Marvin. "Open the windows," she said. "It's stifling in here."

200

Buck took an awkward step toward a window, then stumbled. He was still dazed. Laura opened a window herself.

Whipple stirred, groaned, put hands on the table to push himself upright. Only Kane was still completely out.

Dave's mind revived quicker than his body. He got to his feet and steadied himself against a chair. Something lay on the floor which didn't belong here. It looked like a riding boot.

Lisa saw him staring at it. "That's why we came," she explained. "It was Pinky Ogle's boot and look what we found in it!"

She took a knife from the table and pried between two layers of leather at the rear of the boot top.

"It has a secret hiding place," Laura Kane said.

"And we found this in it," Lisa added as she drew out an old worn envelope. There was a pencilled address on it.

"Did you read it?" Dave asked.

"How could we? It's sealed and addressed to Sheriff Gilroy. He's away in Montana so we brought it to you and Buck."

Blanchard gaped. "What made you look for it?"

"The jailer told us someone slipped in to search Ogle's clothes. So we looked at the boots and they seemed too expensive for Ogle — like they'd been made especially to order."

Dave took the envelope and saw that it had never gone through the mail. There was no postmark or cancellation. The address was:

Adam Gilroy
Sheriff, Salmon City

With a shock he recognized the writing. "It's Gregg's!" he exclaimed. "My brother wrote this."

His hands trembled as he slit the envelope. A single sheet inside had more of Gregg's writing on it. The note was dated October 11, 1878, one day after Gregg had quit the Kaybar to ride south.

Sheriff Gilroy:

I'd lose four days if I rode back to Salmon City to tell you about this. And maybe it don't amount to anything, so I'll just send a note by the first man I meet heading your way. Last night I stopped at a Kaybar line camp with Chuck Spoffard and . . .

Dave skipped down the page to a name. Trego! And a brand. Box Q! At the moment it was more than he could digest but he knew it spelled trouble. Shooting trouble! This was no place for Lisa and Laura.

"Get 'em out of here!" He pushed Lisa toward the door and reached back to drag Laura after him. "Get in that buggy quick and hit for town."

"Not unless we all go," Laura Kane said stubbornly. Her eyes were on Marvin Kane who was at last getting to his feet, still in a stupor.

"Sure we'll all go!" Dave agreed impatiently. "If we don't we're dead ducks. Get 'em ready, Buck, while I go saddle up."

202

He darted through the parlor and out the front door. At the hitchrail were three riding horses and a buggy outfit. Probably the same buggy the two women had driven to the Grady place yesterday. The thing now was to get them started toward town, with the men guarding them.

Kane's horse was saddled but Dave's saddle, and Blanchard's, were draped over the rack. Dave picked up his own saddle, tossed it on and tightened the cinch.

He was reaching for Buck's when he saw Spoffard. Spoffard and eight other men were loping toward the house. A tenth man following at a distance looked like Guiseppe the cook. Dave saw Spoffard jerk a carbine from his saddle scabbard. The others scattered, some breaking to the right, some to the left.

To surround the house! How much had the cook told them? Only that two suspicious sheriffs were here, waiting for them. But a guilty conscience would build on that; clearly it had made them stop the job of bunching cattle and race home.

Two of them looked familiar. Drooping hatbrims kept Dave from being sure; but one of them reminded him of Bushy-Chin and the other looked like Frank Budlong.

At two hundred yards, Spoffard reined to a halt. His carbine whipped level. "Stop right there, Harbison!" he yelled.

Kane's saddle gun was still in its scabbard. Dave snatched it and ran back to the house. Lisa Grady opened the door to let him dive through. As she slammed it shut a bullet splintered the panel. Another shot came from the west and they heard glass shatter in a bedroom. Dave pushed Lisa to a wall. "Keep away from the doors and windows. And stay low, everybody. They're all around us, Buck."

He didn't need to say it for rifle fire was coming from four sides. More window glass shattered. Dave saw Marvin Kane standing in the dining room doorway with a dazed look. "Here's your saddle gun, Kane. Can you use it?"

The man's wits were still foggy and he wasn't yet ready to be mustered for a fight. "How about you, Whipple?" Dave pushed by him to the cattle buyer. A panic held Whipple and he didn't reach for the rifle Dave offered him.

"I'll take it." It was Laura Kane who spoke calmly and took the weapon from Dave. Most of her life she'd been a ranch woman. Dave saw her pump a shell into the chamber and go back to the kitchen with it.

Lisa stood with her back to the parlor wall. "It's a rock house," Dave reminded her. "They can't shoot in on us except through doors and windows." He gave her his six-gun. "Did you ever pull a trigger?"

"Never," she said. "Never in my life."

"Then just shoot for noise when I tell you to. We want 'em to think we've got four guns — one on each side of the house."

Blanchard loomed in front of them. "I made the rounds," he said, shaking his big head to get the grogginess out of it. "Near as I can tell they've got three in the timber on the west side. Three in the bunkhouse and two in the barn. One on the kitchen side and one east of us back of a cordwood pile. Ten in all, countin' the cook."

"Why don't they come at us?" Dave wondered.

Buck smiled grimly. "They would if they knew the shape we're in. They don't know who-all came in the buggy. They don't know Kane's still out on his feet. So they've got to get organized and feel us out."

The parlor clock said five minutes of two. "We've got to keep them leery," Dave said, "till Kane can use a gun. Lisa, when you hear me yell, fire one shot out the front window. Makes no difference whether you hit anything. Just shoot. Buck, you do the same from the west bedroom. Tell Laura to shoot from the kitchen. We all cut loose together when I yell."

"Gotcha," Buck said.

A shot came from the barn and another from the bunk-house. Lisa moved a step toward the parlor's front window. "I'll try," she promised, holding the revolver rigidly in her two hands, her face a mask of determination.

Marvin Kane appeared by Dave with a vacant stare. "Did I see Laura here? Why did she come?"

Dave made him lie on a couch. "You'll be okay in a little while, fella. Then you'll know what to do. Look, I just found out who killed my brother; and it wasn't *you*."

He went back to the covering Whipple and slapped his cheek. "Snap out of it and make yourself useful. If you can't shoot you can look for ammunition. This is a ranchhouse and there's bound to be some shells around. Look for 44–40s. All we've got's what's in the magazines." He gave Whipple a shove.

The dining room had an east window and Dave moved to it. A bullet had already shattered its glass and through the hole Dave saw a cordwood pile with a hat and a rifle barrel showing over it. "Get ready, everybody," he shouted. "Soon as you shoot, Lisa, duck flat on the floor. They'll shoot back. Ready? Go."

Dave aimed at the hat and fired. The hat bounced and disappeared. Buck's rifle cracked from the bedroom and Laura's from the kitchen. Then belatedly a boom from a pistol in the parlor. "Duck!" Dave yelled again.

The woodpile man didn't shoot back. But a fusillade came from the other three sides. More glass shattered and bullets chipped the rock walls.

There was an interval of quiet. Then Whipple came with a box of 44–40s he'd found in a cupboard. "Good work, Whipple." Dave helped himself to a third of them. "Split the rest between Buck and Mrs. Kane."

He went into the parlor and found Kane sitting up, holding his head with both hands. "I had a crazy dream, Harbison. I thought I saw Laura here. Who hit me?"

"The cook hit you with a coffee pot. And Laura *is* here. She's in the kitchen. Steady now! There's a gunfight going on."

Kane gaped. "Who with?"

"With the man who killed my brother down at Hailey. Turns out he had a better reason than yours.

Never mind what, right now. Soon as you feel up to it, go back and help Laura."

The man stared a moment longer. Then he got up and moved with a fairly steady stride toward the kitchen.

Lisa was huddled in a safe corner. Dave gave her a smile of approval and then peered from the parlor window. From it he could see both the bunkhouse and barn. A man in the barn fired over the lower half-door and his bullet hit Dave's sill. As the man stooped out of sight Dave fired a shot through the half-door, hip-high, hoping for a chance hit. A yell told him he'd made one.

Then a shot from the bunkhouse sent a bullet into this room. A picture fell from the parlor wall. Buck's voice shouted from the west bedroom, "Need any help, Lisa?"

"She's all right," Dave called back. "Stick to your post, everybody."

Another short space of quiet. The clock said half past two. It meant six more hours of daylight. And darkness would stiffen the odds against them. At night the besiegers could slip up unseen from four directions.

Dave thought of the envelope found in Ogle's boot. It would be the "proof" he'd hinted at. Dave took it from his pocket and looked again at faded pencil writing made nearly four years ago by Gregg Harbison. During the lull in firing he resumed his reading of it . . .

. . . stopped at a Kaybar line camp, with Chuck Spoffard. Right after supper Chuck rode off to some ranch to sit in a poker game. I was putting out the fire to turn in when a man rode up. He didn't get off his horse. The only light was starlight and I couldn't see him very well. He said: "Message for you, Kruger. From Trego. He says okay it's a deal. If you run for sheriff he'll buy the Box Q and put the title in your name. That way we can . . . Hell, you're not Kruger!" He wheeled his horse and made off. Maybe he was lost and rode into the wrong camp.

I told Chuck about it in the morning. Like me he doesn't know anyone named Trego or Kruger. I'm pass-it along to you though, in case you want to check on it.

Yours,

Gregg Harbison

CHAPTER
TWENTY-ONE

Whipple came in and Dave posted him at the parlor window. "Take a peek every minute or so. If they rush us, sing out."

Then he took the note to the west bedroom and let Buck read it. "The first man Gregg passed on the road, Buck, was Pinky Ogle. A night later Ogle stopped at the Kaybar. There was a squib about it in the paper."

Blanchard narrowed his eyes, nodding. "Pinky steamed the letter open, read it, then sealed it again. He could still deliver it to Gilroy. But by the time he got to town he decided not to."

"He smelled something," Dave agreed, "and hung on to it. He laid low to see who'd buy the Box Q and who'd run for sheriff."

"Nobody bought it," Buck said. "And nobody but Gilroy ran for sheriff. Not that year."

"They were afraid to, Buck, after that bungle at the line camp. So they waited till the next election, two years later. And just to make sure Gregg Harbison didn't hear about it, and put two and two together, they killed him. Likely the killer was Spoffard himself, on his way to Denver. He had to go to Denver, and pretend to make a clean-up gambling, before he could show up in

Salmon City rich enough to buy a top-notch cow ranch. With Gregg out of the way Spoffard wasn't afraid to take title and run for sheriff."

"Gilroy beat him that year," Buck said, "so this year he's running again."

"And to cinch his election, Buck, he goes all out to make Gilroy look bad. Holds up a reprieve so Ad'll hang an innocent man. Frames a bear hunt so proof'll show up too late. Even has someone toss a brick through my window; anything to muddle things up and make Gilroy look like a chump."

"But where does the Box Q fit in?" Buck puzzled. "Trego was no stockman; he was a sneak gold dust raider; him and his whole gang."

"The dust was no good to them," Dave suggested, "unless they could invest it. The best investment in sight was the Box Q. But outlaws like Trego can't put a title on record; so they picked Spoffard for a front. The ranch gave 'em a headquarters to operate from; and with Spoffard as sheriff they could raid high and handsome all over the county."

"Then why," Buck wondered, "are they selling out to Whipple?"

Dave cocked an ear toward the parlor. Silence there meant no immediate threat from that side. "According to this note," Dave answered as he rolled a cigarette, "the head crook was someone named Trego. A few days ago he got himself shot dead at Yellowjacket. About the same time one of them named Fergie got lynched at Leesburg. And there was the hidden proof of Pinky

Ogle's that nobody could find; it was hanging over them all the time."

Buck nodded. "So they got itchy and told Spoffard to cash in. Put what Guiseppe heard on top of that, and they'd be dead sure we're on to 'em. I tracked one of 'em to the river close by here, remember?"

From the few glimpses he'd had of the raiders, Dave felt sure that only two of them were stock hands. The others looked like mining camp hoodlums. Among them would be the man who'd shot Pinky Ogle.

"But we're still missing a bet, somewhere," Dave thought. "They're taking too big a chance, trying to wipe us all out like this. Somebody might come out from town. So why don't they just hightail for the hills?"

They'd be giving up the cattle money and the ranch. But their necks would be safer. It was a big risk to delay here long enough to smoke out six people. If the wind changed the shooting might be heard from a downriver ranch.

"I made it fresh, boys. I mean I didn't just warm up Guiseppe's." Laura Kane stood by them with two steaming cups of coffee.

"Thanks." Dave took one and Buck the other. "Where's Marvin?"

"Holding down the kitchen. It's quiet there now."

"Who knows you and Lisa came out here?"

"Only the jailer," Laura told them. "We rented the same buggy we had yesterday, meaning to finish revamping Mr. Grady's ranchhouse. But first Lisa wanted to say good morning to him so we stopped at

211

the jail. Sweeney told us about a search through Ogle's clothes so we looked at them ourselves. When we found the bootleg letter we thought we'd better come straight to you with it."

Dave frowned. "So only the jailer knows you're here! He'll get worried, won't he, when you don't come back by dark?"

Laura didn't think so. "He'll suppose we've gone directly to the hotel. And the livery people will think we're staying all night at the Grady ranch. We didn't pass anyone on the road." She went back to the kitchen to get coffee for Lisa and Whipple.

Dave looked from Buck's window and saw a timbered slope only a short rifle range away. A man's shoulder showed back of a tree. Dave took aim at it and his bullet chipped bark from the tree's bole. Immediately a return fire came from all sides of the house.

Dave hurried first to Lisa. She sat forlornly on the parlor couch holding a heavy six-shooter. He took it away from her and gave it to Whipple. "Take over the woodpile window, Whipple, and leave this one to me."

A glance over the sill showed no life at either bunkhouse or barn. Lisa spoke from the couch. "What will they do to us, Dave?"

"Nothing, honey, if you keep that pretty head of yours out of sight. Meantime you better be the coffee girl so Laura can use a gun."

Lisa went to the kitchen and for a while Dave was alone in the parlor. A half hour went by without a shot being fired. Then Whipple came in empty-handed.

Laura Kane had taken over his gun and his middle room window. "That woodpile's still got a man behind it," he told Dave.

"They figure to keep us penned up till dark," Dave guessed, "and then rush us. Look, Whipple; you did a pretty good job hunting cartridges. Now start hunting money; or gold dust. Those guys've been raiding placer claims, for years. They'd have to have a cache somewhere. Might be right in this house."

The cattle buyer left the room and was back in ten minutes. "The kitchen has a floor door," he reported. "You can lift it by an iron ring. A grub cellar, maybe."

"Take a lamp and go down there. See what you can find."

This time Whipple was away half an hour. During it not a single shot came from the bunkhouse or barn. Lisa appeared in the parlor with sandwiches and coffee. It was three o'clock.

"Maybe they've gone," Lisa said hopefully.

"Maybe." But Dave knew they hadn't. Shooting too much before the final rush might do them more harm than good; it might be heard by some distant rangeman who'd give an alarm.

Whipple came in to report: "The cellar has eight sacks of potatoes and a keg of whisky. And a big brass trunk. The trunk's locked."

"How heavy is it?"

"I didn't try lifting it. Shall I?"

Lisa was frightened enough already and Dave waited till she continued on her round with food and coffee before he answered. Then: "Might be full of the dust they've been raiding the last few years. If it is, we know why they have to smoke us out. Go down and heave on that trunk. Don't try to crack it open. Just heave on it."

While Whipple went again to the cellar, Dave heard a few shots from the timbered hillside and answering shots from Buck Blanchard. In other directions the besiegers were quiet.

Presently Whipple came back. "Something heavier than duds in that trunk. Want me to . . ."

"Hold on a minute." Dave was peering over the sill. "Someone's coming. Man on a horse. Looks kind of familiar. Go stand guard at Buck's window and send Buck in here."

Blanchard came promptly from the west room. "That shooting you heard," he told Dave, "was to cover a shift they just made. Two of those jiggers in the timber circled to the barn. Leaves only one man on the west. You've got the hot corner, pardner. Three in the bunkshack and four in the barn."

"And one coming in through the gate. Take a look, Buck."

Buck peered out at the oncomer. "He's dressed like a banker," he muttered. "No gun on him. Danged if it ain't Matt Garside the broker. The one that's been tryin' to sell Laura Kane's mine down at Shoup."

It was too late to warn the man. He was now passing the bunkhouse and the outlaws could easily shoot him from the saddle.

Instead, a looped rope was tossed suddenly from the bunkhouse door. The loop fell neatly around Garside. A breath later the man was jerked from the saddle. Dave saw the wolfer Budlong in the doorway pulling on the rope, dragging the broker to him.

He took aim at Budlong but before he could shoot a burst of fire came from the barn. Bullets plowed the sill and a splinter stung Dave's cheek. It spoiled his aim and his shot went wild.

By then they'd pulled Garside out of sight into the bunkhouse. "Why didn't they gun him, Buck?"

"He's worth more to 'em alive," Buck reckoned. "Gives 'em a blue chip to play with."

"Ask Laura if she knows a reason for him to come out here."

Blanchard went to consult Laura Kane. "It figures," he told Dave when he came back. "She hasn't seen him for a week. He's been down at Shoup showing the mine to some investors. If he closed the deal he'd want to tell her about it right away."

It made sense, Dave agreed. From the jailer Garside could learn that Laura had driven a buggy to the Box Q. Apparently he'd followed to report on the deal at Shoup.

"They dassent leave anyone to tell tales on 'em," Buck muttered. "Makes seven of us they gotta snuff out."

"Better check the kitchen, Buck, while I watch the front."

The mantel clock struck four as Blanchard left the parlor. Nearly five hours of daylight yet. Five hours for men with guns, and in force, to come out from town. Dave racked his brain but could think of no reason why they should. And after dark the defenders could easily

215

be rushed from four sides and wiped out. Only by wiping them out could the raiders save their necks.

Just beyond rifle range Dave saw a horseman. He'd left the rear of the barn and was shifting in a wide deep circle to the bunkhouse. Except when out of range the man kept an out-building between himself and Dave's window. By his horse and his hat Dave knew he was Chuck Spoffard.

Spoffard must have seen Budlong drag in a hostage. So he was joining the bunkhouse garrison for a powwow.

"Makes four in the bunkhouse now," Dave said when Buck rejoined him. "They're in a huddle over Garside."

"Kitchen's quiet," Buck reported.

Dave watched the clock while twenty minutes went by. Then he saw Matt Garside, coatless and disheveled, catapult from the bunkhouse. He'd been shoved out and landed in a sprawl.

Rifles bristling from bunkhouse and barn could easily have riddled him. But they didn't. Panic streaked the broker's face as he got to his feet. He staggered a few steps, looked over his shoulder, then ran frantically toward the house.

No bullets followed him. Dave opened the door and let him plunge into the parlor. For a moment he lay panting on the floor. As he got slowly up Buck demanded, "What the hell's goin' on?"

"I'm a flag of truce!" Garside's laugh had hysteria in it as he backed to the couch and sat down. "That's what Spoffard called me; a white flag with a message."

"You mean they're offerin' a deal?"

Garside ran a tongue around his lips. "They say you can take it or leave it. Take it and live, Houcks says, or leave it and die."

"Who's Houcks?"

"Never saw him before. But I heard them call him that. Kruger's the name they call Spoffard. Houcks gives the orders. While they argued about terms I heard him say: 'Shut up, Kruger; until we picked you up you were just a forty dollar cowhand.'"

Lisa Grady was standing round-eyed in the inner doorway. Whipple's pale face looked over her shoulder and Dave snapped, "Get back to your window, Whipple."

"What's the deal?" Blanchard asked impatiently.

"They'll ride away and leave us all unharmed, Houcks says, on two conditions."

"Yeah? What are they?"

"First is that we bring up what's in a cellar trunk. Here's the trunk key." Garside produced a brass key and gave it to Blanchard. "There's a wheelbarrow on the back porch. We put the stuff in it. It's in thirty small canvas bags and Houcks says altogether it weighs about a hundred and thirty pounds."

Dave whistled. "That much dust," he estimated, "would come to around thirty thousand dollars! What's his second condition?"

"They want one hostage to take with 'em. If we keep our mouths shut till they get a day's ride away, they'll turn the hostage loose. Any man of us'll do, Houcks says. He's to walk out unarmed and wheel that loaded

217

barrow to the barn. If it happens by five o'clock we can live; if it doesn't, we can't."

Every eye went to the clock. It was half past four.

Dave looked at Lisa and made a hard bitter choice. Any price in gold was cheap if it would save her life. "We'll say yes to the first condition," he decided, "and no to the second. They can have their dust but nix on a hostage. They'd gun him, once they got him off in the woods. What do you say, Buck?"

"I say the same," Buck agreed promptly. "Let 'em take their stealings and run; but we don't chip in any blood." He looked at Lisa and saw Laura appear beside her. "If we were all men I wouldn't even give 'em the dust," Blanchard added grimly. "I'd say to hell with 'em."

"Just a minute, Blanchard!" Marvin Kane came suddenly into the parlor. "And listen, Harbison. We want to save these girls, don't we? Anything's worth that, isn't it? To me it is." He went to the front window, leaned through it and shouted: "Okay, Houcks. We accept the terms. I'm your hostage. Be with you just as quick as I can load up."

He turned to Blanchard and snatched the trunk key from his hand. "Get out of my way, Buck. I'm taking them up on it and you can't stop me."

CHAPTER
TWENTY-TWO

Dave caught up with him in the kitchen. The floor door there was still propped open, after Whipple's two trips to the cellar. Kane, trunk key in hand, was starting down the steps when Dave pulled him back. "You damned fool! What do you think you're doing?" He kicked the door and it fell level with the floor.

"I told you what I'm doing. Get out of my way." The Kaybar man twisted free from Dave's grip and reached down for the floor ring.

"You're outvoted, Kane." Again Dave pulled him away. "The rest of us won't stand for it." He took the key from Kane's hand.

"Of course we won't, Marvin." It was Laura Kane who appeared beside them. Before she could say more a rifle cracked outside and a bullet splattered plaster from the kitchen wall. For the last few minutes the post here had been unmanned.

"A wonder they haven't busted in on us!" Dave exclaimed angrily. "Get back to your window, Kane. Laura, I'll have Garside take over yours."

Kane glared rebelliously. "We've got till five o'clock, that's all!" he protested hoarsely. "What are you going to do about it?"

"We'll scrap it out with 'em," Dave said.

Kane picked up his rifle and stood at the kitchen window. And Laura, gazing at him, had a look in her eyes which wasn't censure. *He's not hurting himself with her,* Dave thought. Aloud he said to her: "This makes twice the damned fool's tried to get his head blown off; once with Tracy Smith and now with these Houcks gunnies."

He took her to the middle room window and then went looking for Garside. "Any good with a gun?" he asked the broker.

"Never fired one in my life." The man was still limp from shock.

It put him in a class with Whipple. Neither could be counted on in a fight. "Okay. Then stand by Mrs. Kane and act as a lookout for her. You do the peeking and she'll do the shooting."

When Garside was posted Dave made an inspection in the west room. Whipple was there peering fearfully out at a wooded slope. "See anyone?" Dave asked him.

The man turned his pale moist face to Dave. "Not now. A minute ago I saw that Italian cook." The cattle buyer stared bleakly at the pistol in his hand. "I couldn't hit anything with this."

"You can make a noise with it," Dave said. There were only three rifles, Blanchard's, Kane's and his own.

Rejoining Blanchard he looked at the parlor clock. It lacked fifteen minutes of five. "If they don't rush us at five, Buck, they won't till dark."

"How's Kane? Behavin' himself?"

"He's been hating himself," Dave said, "for the last two years. Ever since he figured wrong about Gregg

220

and Laura. Now he's doing his damnedest to make up for it."

Buck grinned. "Sackcloth and ashes, the preachers call it."

Dave looked warily out at the bunkhouse whose windows showed four steel barrels. One of them spat a bullet aimed not to hit but to warn. A bellicose voice followed it. "Your time's runnin' out, up there!"

According to the ultimatum, in just ten minutes a hostage should start wheeling a laden barrow toward the barn. When it didn't happen there'd be a fury of disappointment and impatience. Some of the outlaws would want to close in at once.

Dave made another round of the house, found all lookouts alert. In a bedroom he came upon Lisa rummaging through the drawers of a dresser. "I feel so useless, Dave. Maybe I can find something; maybe another box of shells . . ."

"That's fine, honey. Maybe you can locate some bandages or medicine, in case somebody gets shot up. Stay out of the parlor. *And don't give up.*"

"Dad didn't." She turned with a question. "The Richmires should be in Virginia City by now, shouldn't they?"

Dave made a calculation. "Let's see. This is Saturday. They got to Red Rock Thursday evening. If they made connections with a train there they could leave Dillon early Friday. And they'd've had all day Saturday to look at Bert Stanky."

He kissed her and went back to Blanchard. The clock said four minutes to five. This was the side of greatest threat, with seven of the ten raiders concentrated in bunkhouse and barn.

"If they come at us, Buck, you take the bunkshack crowd and I'll take the barn. Do you know Houcks by sight?"

Buck didn't. "Garside says he's wide and short. Doeskin jacket and denim pants. I'll down him first; then Spoffard; then Budlong."

A metallic ticking taunted them as the last minutes slipped by. Then came five mellow chimes as the clock struck the hour.

As the last note sounded, rifles cracked from all sides of the house. A hail of bullets swept into the parlor. Dave heard a shout from Houcks. "You had your chance, Sheriff!"

Dave raised his chin to the sill level and yelled back. "You'd better take yours, Houcks. If you start now, you can be out of the county by morning."

"And leave you to peach on us!" Houcks jeered. "We'd be crazy." He fired again and Dave got his head down just in time.

"They're bound to figger it that way," Buck reasoned. "They've gone a sight too far to dig out and leave any witnesses."

"A sight too far!" Dave agreed. "When you ride a trail like theirs, you've got to cover your tracks and keep going."

"Like a river of no return!" the voice behind them was Lisa's. It had a tone of hollow despair as she added, "I think Mr. Kane's been hit, Dave."

222

As he hurried to the rear Dave saw that Laura had left her middle room window. Garside was there, unarmed and peering out at the woodpile. Dave kept on to the kitchen and found Laura giving first aid to an arm wound. Marvin Kane sat in a chair with his teeth clenched against pain. "Hand me that kettle, Dave," Laura said. Kane's sleeve had blood on it and she cut it away.

Lisa, making ready for trouble like this, had put a kettle of salt water on the stove. From a cabinet she'd assembled iodine, court plaster and bandages. Laura soaked a rag and bathed a bullet-chipped arm. "Hold still, Marvin." She wound the bandage snugly.

"She's done it before," the rancher said faintly to Dave.

Dave looked from the kitchen window and saw no threat of attack. There would be, though, if the outlaws knew they'd winged Kane. They'd charge from the east, too, if they knew only an unarmed broker was watching that side. Dave hurried to Garside, fired a warning shot at the cordwood pile, then rushed to Whipple on the opposite side of the house.

Whipple, his face milk white, was crouching under his window. "Are they coming?" he asked hoarsely.

Dave shook him. "Why don't you look out and see? No, they're not coming right now. But they'd be in here already if they knew what a funk you're in. Okay. I'll take over here. Go join Garside and maybe you can buck each other up."

Dave himself, during the next hour, kept circling the house. He didn't dare stay at any one spot more than a minute. As he passed each post he fired his rifle from it, with or without a target. He must make them think each side of the house had a rifleman guard.

Actually only the front side had an effective defense. A charge there would run into deadly fire from Blanchard. The two white-collar men, Garside and Whipple, would be worth nothing in a showdown. And except for Dave's intermittent visits to it, the west window was unmanned.

In the kitchen the Kanes had traded weapons. Laura now had the rifle and Marvin, his left arm burning with pain, had the hand gun. A strange reunion, Dave thought. Laura stood at the window with her back to Marvin. From a chair by the stove Kane said: "Quiet as a church on this side, Harbison."

"Cut loose if they come at you," Dave said. "It won't be till dark, likely."

He rejoined Blanchard at the front, told him about the Kanes. "Do you reckon he'll get her back, Buck?"

"If he does," Buck thought, "he'll be doin' it the hard way. And all for nothing, unless we get help by nightfall."

A shot from the woodpile made Dave join Garside and Whipple. "I took a peek," Garside told him, "and got shot at." He had considerably more spine than Whipple.

"So you're lucky," Dave said. "Your luck'll run out if you don't keep watching."

He continued the rounds, found the Kanes quiet and alert. A pot was boiling and Kane used his good hand to refuel the stove.

Just as Dave returned to the parlor the clock struck six. "The bunkshack's playing 'possum," Buck said. "Not a peep from 'em since you left."

"It's near sundown, Buck. When does it get dark?"

"It won't get inky dark till around nine o'clock."

The raiders would need pitch darkness, Dave reasoned, to attack with a certainty of success. Two or three men could come simultaneously from four directions. They'd arrive unseen at the outer walls. At close range they'd shoot locks from the doors and come swarming at the windows. Some of the entrances would be undefended.

"We can make 'em pay heavy for it," Buck growled. "Maybe if we pile up the first three or four the others'll run."

Dave doubted it. For all the outlaws knew, they'd already killed one or more of the defenders. They'd hang no higher if they did for the rest. Certainly they'd gone too far to do anything else than cover their tracks and keep going. For men with their record it was a trail of no return.

Nor would they be willing to desert thirty thousand dollars' worth of loot in a cellar trunk.

Dave continued on from post to post as the minutes crawled by. At six-thirty the light was still bright outside.

At six-forty it began to dim a little. At six-fifty Lisa brought a pot of coffee to the parlor.

For half an hour not a shot had been fired by the raiders. Only a cool, still twilight seemed to rule the world outside; that and the mellow whistle of a whippoorwill as it wheeled across the sky.

Again Lisa took hope. "Maybe they've gone, Dave."

"Maybe." But he knew they hadn't.

"They never did unsaddle their broncs," Buck said. "Tied 'em back of the corral. I'll look and see if they're still there."

He leaned from the window, craning his neck to see a row of mounts tied beyond the corral.

It drew a shot from the bunkhouse. Both Dave and Lisa saw Buck Blanchard meet the shock of a bullet, heard his knees bump the floor, saw his big hands grip the sill to keep from falling.

"They got me, pardner!" It was barely a whisper and the last word the man ever spoke. A breath later he'd lost his grip on the sill. His big frame lay face-down under the window with a pool of blood forming around his head.

Lisa stood with hands over her mouth, staring down at him. The horror of it left her dumb. Dave took a quick look, saw that it was a brain hit. Buck Blanchard had fought his last fight. In a minute more he'd be dead.

Dave said huskily, "Don't let them know, Lisa!" He meant the outlaws. They didn't yet know they'd killed the house's strongest arm of defense. If they knew they wouldn't even wait till dark. Making them wait was the only thin hope now, and every minute counted.

Dave made sure they weren't coming; then he stood back and put an arm around Lisa. She was on the ragged edge of fainting. "Remember what you said, honey; your dad didn't give up so why should we?"

The girl stood trembling against him, her face to his shoulder. "But what can we do?" It had been bad enough before; now it was infinitely more hopeless.

"They won't come till dark, honey. Black dark. By then maybe we'll get help from town."

When she went to tell the Kanes, Dave moved Buck from under the window and put a blanket over him. The big deputy had stopped breathing. Dave picked up his rifle, checked both it and his own to make sure the magazines were full. When they rushed him he could pump twelve fast shots.

But they'd be too smart to rush him while there was good shooting light. Right now Dave could see no sign of them. They were waiting for black darkness. The clock said two minutes before seven. Inky darkness wouldn't come before nine. Was there any possible reason why honest men should ride out here, in force, during the next two hours?

Not a chance, Dave thought dismally. Not a dim ghost of a chance that they'd come, in force and in time!

CHAPTER
TWENTY-THREE

Jake Slavin's stage from Red Rock was on schedule. At two minutes before seven he turned into Main Street and trotted his four-in-hand toward the hotel. Always his arrival was an event and usually a crowd waited for him on the hotel walk.

For if any news came from a world beyond the Bitterroots the stage from Red Rock was sure to bring it first. Some day, when they got telegraph wires here, it would be different. But now only Jake Slavin or his passengers could possibly know the latest from points along the railroad.

This evening four people in particular were sure to meet his stage with eager questions. As usual it gave Slavin an expansive feeling, a sense of importance.

But when he stopped at the hotel, only one of the four was there.

That one was Judge Corry. The Grady girl wasn't in sight; neither were the two deputies, Blanchard and Harbison.

A livery hostler took charge of the stage and Slavin joined Corry on the walk. The judge, like everyone else in town, knew that Jake had spent Thursday driving from here to Red Rock, Friday resting at Red Rock, and Saturday driving back to Salmon City.

"What about the Richmires?" Corry inquired guardedly. Only he himself, the county attorney, the sheriff's force and Lisa Grady knew about the expedition to Virginia City. And until now, there'd been no way of knowing its progress.

"They got to Red Rock," Jake said, "about an hour after dark Thursday night."

"Then they missed the train to Dillon!" The judge concluded.

"Yeh, but a freight came along and they rode the caboose. Saved 'em a full day. Yesterday the Dillon operator told us they caught the Friday stage for Virginia City. He said the Richmires were rarin' for a look at that guy."

"Humph!" The judge seemed pleased. "They made good time. So they should be on their way back by now."

But why, Jake puzzled, wasn't Lisa Grady here to ask the same question? She, far more than anyone else, would want to know whether the Richmires were behind or ahead of schedule.

He inquired for her at the hotel desk. "Haven't seen her since morning," the clerk said.

Since he couldn't tell Lisa he could at least pass the news on to Court Grady. So Slavin walked a block to the jail.

Pop Sweeney let him into the cell corridor where he spoke to the prisoner. "Catchin' that freight saved 'em a lot of time," Jake finished, "so it won't be long now."

"Have you told Lisa?" Grady asked him.

"Can't seem to find her anywhere."

The jailer was standing by. "Along about noontime she drove out to the Box Q," he said. "Her and Mrs. Kane."

Slavin cocked an eyebrow. "The Box Q? What took 'em out there?"

"Buck Blanchard and young Harbison are there. Lisa wanted to show 'em somethin' she found in Pinky Ogle's boot."

The eyebrow arched higher. "Found what in a boot?"

"An old envelope addressed to Gilroy. It was sealed and they didn't open it; just took it out to them deputies. They'd rid out to the Box Q earlier, Buck and Dave had; what for I don't know. Likely they're all back by now. Likely they're at the hotel eatin' supper."

But Slavin knew better. If they were in town they would have met the stage for news of the Richmires.

It mystified Jake but at the moment didn't worry him. Whatever was delaying the two women, they were in good company. Buck and Dave would see them home all right. Chuck Spoffard was a hearty host and probably he'd talked them into staying for supper.

Which reminded Jake that he'd had no supper himself; nor the pick-up drink he usually had right after a stage run. So he crossed to Pope's bar for a quick one.

The place was crowded and a glance told Jake why. Pope, the proprietor, was counting ballots. They were an accumulation of straw votes he'd dumped from a box onto the bar. The bartender was keeping tally as

230

Pope called them one by one. "Spoffard; Gilroy; Gilroy; Spoffard; Spoffard; Spoffard." Pope looked up from his ballots. "Seems like Chuck's runnin' ahead two to one."

It was Saturday night, Jake remembered — a time long planned for the tabbing of this poll. For a month customers had been dropping tickets in a box, one vote per drink, with Chuck Spoffard often standing treat to promote his own showing.

So why wasn't Chuck here at the finish? Having boomed himself for weeks, treating lavishly at this bar, why wasn't he here to bask in his triumph?

Why? It made *two* people who weren't where they should be. Lisa Grady and Chuck Spoffard!

Trouble was stirring and Jake Slavin felt it in his bones. He went out on the sidewalk and stopped the first cowboy who came along. He was Rufe Barrow, a Mulkey hand. "How many of your outfit are in town, Rufe?"

Rufe grinned. "It's Saturday night, ain't it? So we're *all* in town."

The two Barrock brothers from the Big Triangle ranch came by and Jake beckoned them. "Listen, boys." It took only a minute to tell what was on his mind. "That boot could have murder proof in it. Maybe it got those gals into trouble. Let's fan out there and see."

Jim Barrock nodded thoughtfully. "Maybe we'd better. It's only six-seven miles."

"I'll round up our outfit," Rufe Barrow said. "There comes Phil Shenon; and Wes Gordon of the Kaybar. Maybe they'll go along too."

Saddled mounts were at the hitchrails. Presently seven men loped out of town, taking the upriver trail.

The twilight faded slowly. From the front there'd been no firing since seven o'clock but right after seven-thirty Dave heard a burst of fire at the rear. Five rifle shots directed at the kitchen. They were echoed by shots from the east and the west. His own post, facing the bunkhouse and barn, continued quiet.

He was debating whether to go back there when Lisa came into the parlor. He'd told her to stay out of this death room, where Blanchard lay under a blanket and where the brunt of attack should come.

"Marvin thinks it's a trick, Dave," Lisa said. "A trick to make you leave here."

"It figures," Dave muttered. One raider on each of the other sides could make plenty of noise while the main force lay doggo in front. "Is Kane still in the kitchen?"

"No. He went to the west room."

"Good." It gave them at least a lookout on all fronts. Dave glanced at the clock but in the dimming light could barely see the hands. They were so nearly together that he knew it was about twenty minutes to eight. "Better get out of here, Lisa."

She left him and Dave kept at his post, peering over the sill. The sky was cloudless; but it was half a month past full moon. So the first hours of night would have no light but starlight.

A man wearing an old cavalryman's hat, with a chin strap, showed briefly at the barn door. He made a fair

232

target but Dave didn't shoot. Maybe they thought he'd gone to the back of the house and would come charging in force. He must be ready to pick them off. They didn't know they'd killed Blanchard. Nor could they know for certain who'd come in the buggy. The buggy horse, head drooping, still stood at the hitchrack. At the same rack were three saddle horses. Garside's mount, reins hanging, stood free near the well trough.

The raiders would know, of course, that a loose horse in the corral was Whipple's. They'd know that the hitchrack horses were Kane's, Harbison's and Blanchard's. They wouldn't know, though, that Garside had no gun skill.

The mantel clock sounded eight and still no firing from barn or bunkhouse. Occasional shots from the other directions were decoy shots, Dave thought.

Lisa came again with a message from Kane. Only the Italian cook was on the west, Kane thought; and only one seemed to be back of the east woodpile. "Two were on the kitchen side an hour ago; but Laura thinks one of them has gone — a man wearing an old army hat."

"He shifted to the barn, Lisa." It made Dave surer than ever that the real onset would come from the front.

The shapes of barn and bunkhouse grew dimmer. At eight-thirty Dave could still see them but at eight-forty-five he couldn't. He couldn't even see Lisa when she came next from the kitchen. This time she didn't speak. But he knew she was there, standing in the inner doorway back of him.

Dread for her preyed on him and made him talk. "I guess you know how I feel about you, Lisa."

"Tell me," she said.

"If we get out of this I'd want us to get married. *Would* you?"

"Yes."

He almost missed the one low-spoken word as another sound came from close outside his window. A crackle of gravel under a boot. Dave punched his rifle through the window and fired. In the flash he saw the shape of a man and fired again.

A few inches beyond the front door a six-gun boomed three times and a lock shattered. By then Dave was in mid-room, shooting and shouting. "Blast 'em, Buck!" He must make them think Blanchard was still siding him. Buck's pistol was in his right hand and his left held a rifle. He triggered the short gun at the door just as someone kicked it open.

CHAPTER
TWENTY-FOUR

A body fell across the threshold. Dave pushed Lisa into the middle room and flung himself flat on the parlor floor. Bullets streamed through the window and open door, zinging over Dave to thud on the wall. Dave heard shooting from the kitchen and from the west room; a whimper of panic came from Whipple.

Above all this Dave heard something else. A pounding of hooves as horsemen raced this way. A shout splitting the night didn't come from the raiders. A friendly shout! "You in there, Buck?"

A high-pitched voice sounded like. Jake Slavin's. "What's goin' on in there? What happened to them women?"

Then a hoarse, guarded voice nearer the door. "Let's get outa here, Lucas." Dave thought it was Chuck Spoffard.

He heard men stampeding toward the corral. It was a retreat, sudden and pell mell. Dave gave a yell of triumph, got up, lunged through the doorway and tripped over a body there. He scrambled to his feet and plunged blindly on through the dark, pursuing sounds, collided with a horseman who'd pulled up in front. "That you, Buck?" The voice was Wes Gordon's of the Kaybar.

"No. I'm Harbison. Go into the house and help Laura Kane."

Dave dashed on and bumped into the poles of a corral. Beyond the corral he heard prancings, snorts, cursings; the outlaws were tightening cinches, swinging into saddles. "Stop 'em!" Dave yelled. He whipped up his rifle and fired at sound.

A squeal meant he'd hit horseflesh. Guns blazed back at him and in the flashes Dave saw mounted men. They were shooting at him as they wheeled, spurring off into darkness.

"Wait for me!" The cry was Spoffard's and Dave fired at the sound of it. Spoffard who'd been left behind beside a fallen, bullet-bit horse! The shot drew return fire and in the flash Dave glimpsed him, standing alone beyond the corral. "Wait for me!" the deserted man cried again.

But no one waited for him. Hoofbeats of the others faded out.

What would he do? He had two choices, Dave reasoned. He could dash away afoot, in a hopeless flight, and be easily tracked down in the morning. Or he could get himself another horse right now.

Dave leaned his rifle against the poles. Then he climbed quietly over them armed only with a six-gun. He was inside the corral now — a corral containing one loose horse — Whipple's. All day Whipple's saddle had been in plain sight, draped over the corral fence not far to Dave's left.

Guiding himself by the poles, Dave moved softly that way. Step by cautious step. After a dozen steps his groping hand touched leather. A saddle. If he was guessing right, Spoffard would be slipping stealthily toward it from the opposite direction.

And he'd need to hurry. A pandemonium of talk, confused questions and hysterical answers, came from up near the house. Dave heard Kane's jubilant voice, "They're on the run, Laura!" Then a question from Lisa, "Where are you, Dave?"

He couldn't shout back. If he did he'd lose Spoffard. Spoffard who was the bitter root of it all! The man who'd stopped by Hailey, on his way to Denver two years ago, to shoot down Gregg Harbison!

Dave's left hand was touching the saddle when he felt it move. Someone was tugging at it, lifting it from the fence.

"You're not going anywhere," Dave said. His gun was breast level.

The saddle thumped on the ground as both men fired, Dave shifting sideways as he squeezed his trigger. The range was point blank, so close that he felt a burn at his cheek. He tripped his trigger once more, felt a jolt as Spoffard toppled against him. A little way off in the dark Whipple's horse gave a snort as it shied across the corral.

Again a cry from the house. "Where are you, Dave?"

And this time he could answer. "Here I am, Lisa. Coming!"

That was Saturday night. On Sunday Dave was too exhausted to join a posse giving chase to the surviving outlaws. On Monday, with hundreds of others, he attended

237

the burial of Buck Blanchard. Tuesday morning he slept late and was wakened by a noise of hammering.

A clock by his bed said ten, and a calendar on the wall told the date. Until he was fully awake, the date and the hour gave him a strangely uneasy feeling. Then, remembering, he relaxed. This was the thirtieth day since he'd raced into town with a telegram. The last day and the final hour of a thirty-day reprieve.

But it didn't matter now, Dave knew as he got up to dress leisurely. He bathed and shaved, then stood at his window to look up the street. From here he could see the source of the hammering. In the jailyard, a block up Main, they were dismantling a scaffold built to hang Court Grady.

It wouldn't be needed now. For late last night a buckboard had arrived from Montana bearing Gilroy, the county attorney and an elderly couple named Richmire. They'd brought joyful news for Court and Lisa Grady — news which had kept the entire town up half the night celebrating. "We made a mistake," the Richmires said. And the county attorney said: "Since it's supported by the evidence found up Geerston Gulch, let's call it a mistrial."

Waiving aside all procedural delays, Judge Corry had promptly agreed.

A little after midnight a cell door had opened to let Court Grady walk out into the arms of his daughter. The street was full, even at that late hour. Men who'd assembled to see him hanged, thirty days ago, last night had swarmed over him with cheers and good wishes.

238

To avoid another crowd at the hotel, and to give the Gradys a quiet privacy of reunion, Marvin Kane had offered them his backstreet cottage for the night. They were resting there now, Dave supposed.

Someone knocked at his door and he opened it to admit Ad Gilroy. The sheriff looked gray and haggard, yet there was a spring in his step as he came in and sat on the bed.

"Any word from the posse?" Dave asked him.

"They lost the sign," Gilroy reported as he stoked his pipe, "somewhere 'tother side of Williams Creek Pass. But now we get a break from that cook Guiseppe."

"Yeh?" Dave knew of course that all but three of the Box Q raiders had gotten away in the dark. Two were dead. Houcks had been dropped on the front door threshold and Spoffard in the corral. Guiseppe, afoot with a leg wound, had been picked up in the woods.

"If we go easy on him," Gilroy said, "he'll tip us to where the hideaway is. It's near the top of Mahoney Creek, he claims, west of Middle Fork and beyond the Yellowjacket wilderness. Says he'll lead us right to it if we promise not to hang him."

"Sounds like a fair trade." Dave held a match to the sheriff's pipe. "What about that trunkful of dust?"

"We hauled it to town. Judge Corry thinks we'd better divide it among the Leesburg placer miners who've been raided these last few years. Same goes for the whole Box Q outfit, land and cattle."

Dave nodded. According to the long lost note from Gregg Harbison, the Box Q had been bought with loot.

"The two regular hands, Lucas and Limpy, were in on it, the cook says. Says it was Lucas who sniped Ogle on orders from Chuck Spoffard." Gilroy puffed comfortably a minute. "The county'll have to take over that ranch," he went on. "It's got livestock. And livestock has to be looked after; not next year or next month, but right now. The job's yours, boy, if you want it."

"How long would it last?"

"Until we can hold a public auction and sell it to . . ." Gilroy's eyes narrowed as an idea struck him. "Why not to you, Dave? It's got a good furnished house. You and Lisa could —"

"Don't make me laugh!" Dave cut in. "Where would I get the money?"

"Why not from the bank? Or from Colonel Shoup? Or from those Leesburg miners who'll get back what they lost to Houcks? Lots of money in this valley needs investing. Best investment in the world is a young man with savvy and guts. What's more, you could bid it in cheap. This county owes you a lot, boy; so nobody'd try to outbid you."

"I'll think it over," Dave grinned. "Right now let's go make a bid for breakfast."

They went down to the lobby. The midnight excitement had disrupted the schedule here, so the dining room was still half full. As they paused in the doorway Dave felt a nudge from Gilroy. "There they are; betcha they'll be back on the Kaybar together, before long."

240

Dave saw them, Laura and Marvin Kane, at a small table. This time it was Matt Garside who sat alone across the room. "There's another chance for a loan, boy," Gilroy suggested slyly. "She's just sold a mine and don't know what to do with the money. Let's go say good morning to 'em."

But a voice at Dave's elbow made him turn. The midget bartender Chung was holding forth a small, sealed envelope. "For you, Mr. Dave. It comes by special messenger."

Dave opened it, glanced at a line of writing, then turned to Gilroy. "Reckon you'll have to go in alone, Sheriff. See you later."

He went out and hurried down Main toward the river. Friendly voices hailed him. Pop Sweeney grinned at him from the jail doorway. Pop had only one prisoner now, Guiseppe. But soon there'd be more. One would be Bert Stanky, just as soon as he could be extradited from Montana.

At St. Charles Street Dave turned left and hurried on. Beyond the cottonwoods he heard the rushing river, its breath coming cool and sweet to the life of this mountain morning.

In the second block he came to a cottage with smoke curling from its chimney. This was the Kane town house and Dave Harbison stopped there. The note was still in his hand and he read it again.

Dad and I are having a late family breakfast. Won't you please join us?

Love, Lisa

241

A family! All the loneliness of the years left Dave. He'd lost Gregg, the only family he could remember, and now Lisa was giving him another. Something worth a good deal more than land or gold or livestock — people who wanted him. They were waiting for him in there. Proudly he went up the steps; eagerly he knocked on the door.